VIRTUAL UNIVERS

Oscar Wilde's
The Picture of Dorian Gray

STUDY GUIDE
& WORKBOOK

FREE VIRTUAL CLASSROOM ACCESS

Abby Leigh Hunter, Editor

The Picture of Dorian Gray: Study Guide & Workbook

Copyright © 2020 Virtual University Press
First Edition: July 11, 2020

This volume is a unique and original work protected by copyright under U.S. law and international treaties. No part of this book may be reproduced, uploaded, or shared on any blog, website, social network or other medium, digital, print, or otherwise, without the publisher's express written consent, except for brief quotations embodied in critical articles and reviews.

This interactive study guide and workbook is part of a series designed for the enjoyment of modern readers and for classroom use by English, literature, and writing students. It includes a study guide with chapter summaries, discussion/essay prompts, and chapter-based quizzes with multiple-choice answers, which readers can use to better understand the world's great classics and test their comprehension of key concepts, characters, dialogue, and events in the story.

College bookstores and other educational institutions may place wholesale orders through Ingram Content Group. Students and other readers may purchase single copies in e-book, paperback, and hardcover from online booksellers and brick-and-mortar bookstores. Please refer to the following URLs to locate the current, correct edition of this workbook:

ISBN Numbers:

978-1-64399-022-4	Retail Paperback (Ingram)
978-1-64399-023-1	Retail Hardcover (Ingram)
978-1-64399-026-2	EPUB digital edition

Virtual University Press

Website:	https://books.vu.org
Email:	Editor@VU.org
Phone:	(805) 888-2900
Fax:	(805) 702-2700

Table of Contents

About This Workbook 5
Editor's Foreword 7
The Characters of the Story 13
Chapter 1 Review 17
Chapter 2 Review 19
Chapter 3 Review 21
Chapter 4 Review 23
Chapter 5 Review 27
Chapter 6 Review 31
Chapter 7 Review 33
Chapter 8 Review 37
Chapter 9 Review 41
Chapter 10 Review 43
Chapter 11 Review 47
Chapter 12 Review 51
Chapter 13 Review 55
Chapter 14 Review 59
Chapter 15 Review 63
Chapter 16 Review 65
Chapter 17 Review 69
Chapter 18 Review 71
Chapter 19 Review 75
Chapter 20 Review 77
Further Discussion/Essay Prompts 81
Chapter 1 Quiz: Answers 87
Chapter 2 Quiz: Answers 88
Chapter 3 Quiz: Answers 89
Chapter 4 Quiz: Answers 90

Chapter 5 Quiz: Answers 92

Chapter 6 Quiz: Answers 93

Chapter 7 Quiz: Answers 94

Chapter 8 Quiz: Answers 96

Chapter 9 Quiz: Answers 97

Chapter 10 Quiz: Answers 98

Chapter 11 Quiz: Answers 99

Chapter 12 Quiz: Answers 100

Chapter 13 Quiz: Answers 101

Chapter 14 Quiz: Answers 102

Chapter 15 Quiz: Answers 104

Chapter 16 Quiz: Answers 105

Chapter 17 Quiz: Answers 106

Chapter 18 Quiz: Answers 107

Chapter 19 Quiz: Answers 109

Chapter 20 Quiz: Answers 110

The Elements of Style: Classic Edition (2018)Error! Bookmark not defined.

About This Workbook

This study guide and workbook is designed for classroom use by English, literature, and writing students, as well as for leisure readers desiring deeper insights into Oscar Wilde's literary classic, *The Picture of Dorian Gray*. It includes an editor's introduction that offers rich historical context on the book and insights into the author's life and times; a study guide with brief chapter summaries and discussion prompts; and chapter-based quizzes that readers can use to self-test their understanding of key concepts, characters, and events in the story. Quiz answers are provided in the *Chapter Quiz Answers* section at the back of the book.

This edition also has an interactive component, giving readers online access to a minimalist "virtual classroom" devoted to *The Picture of Dorian Gray,* hosted on the Virtual University Press website. Features of this e-learning environment include:

1. Fully interactive, multiple-choice chapter quizzes with randomized questions, shuffled answers, and auto-scoring in real-time.

2. A Web Resources section with a curated assortment of videos and Web-based study materials.

3. An expanded Vocabulary Guide (launches in Sept. 2020) comprised of 1,000+ frequently misunderstood words, drawn from *The Picture of Dorian* Gray and organized by chapter, with brief definitions and interactive quizzes, auto-scored in real time. Readers cannot appreciate a great book unless they understand the words they are reading, and this vocabulary feature will prove invaluable to readers and students.

Access to this virtual classroom is free to our readers. If prompted for a password, enter: DG2020-JXK9. The website interface is compatible with most modern Web browsers including Chrome (and Chrome variants), Opera, Firefox, and Microsoft Edge.

To access the virtual classroom for *The Picture of Dorian Gray,* browse to: *https://books.vu.org/titles/dorian_gray*

Editor's Foreword

The Picture of Dorian Gray is Wilde's first and only novel. It is arguably his most famous work and one of the most controversial books of the late nineteenth century. Wilde's other writings included a substantial body of plays, poetry, essays, and epigrams (short poems and pithy sayings that express an idea in a clever or amusing way).

Two versions of Wilde's novel exist: an uncensored, 13-chapter story published in 1890, and a 20-chapter revision published a year later. (This workbook covers the 20-chapter version, which is more popular and widely read.) The story initially appeared in the July 1890 issue of Lippincott's Monthly Magazine. The editor was concerned that it would be labeled obscene, so he cut five hundred words from the manuscript without Wilde's knowledge before going to press. Even after these deletions, the gothic tale provoked an uproar in socially conservative, Victorian-era England. Some complained it was indecent, others called for Wilde and the magazine to be criminally prosecuted.

To quell the outrage, Wilde edited his work and published a tamer, 20-chapter version in 1891; but it too was widely condemned as immoral. Wilde added a preface to his edited version espousing his views on creating art for art's sake rather than being constrained by sociopolitical themes.

Oscar Wilde (1882)

He observed, "Those who find ugly meanings in beautiful things are corrupt without being charming...Those who find beautiful meanings in beautiful things are the cultivated." He also declared: "There is no such thing as a moral or an immoral book. Books are well written or badly written. That is all."

The Picture of Dorian Gray is rooted in the oft-used Faustian story line of striking a bargain with the devil, blended with the Narcissus myth from Ovid's *Metamorphoses*. The story centers around an extraordinarily handsome young man named Dorian Gray. A painter (Basil Hallward) awakens Dorian's vanity by painting a stunning portrait of the young man. As he admires the portrait, which captures the essence of his youth and beauty, Dorian is moved to say that he would give his soul if he could remain eternally young, while the painting grows old. Wilde makes no mention of Dorian negotiating a Faustian contract, and the reader is left to assume that it happened at some point. From there, the story follows the customary exchange of one's soul for earthly pleasures.

Early on, Dorian becomes inspired by Lord Henry Wotton and falls under his influence. Lord Henry is an unbridled hedonist who believes that the pursuit of beauty through sensual pleasure should be elevated above morality. His views reflect the philosophy of aestheticism and the Decadent movement, which had begun to influence artistic and literary thought in the late nineteenth-century (and which Wilde wholeheartedly embraced in his own life). When Dorian's verbalized wish for eternal youth is granted, the painting begins to age while his physical appearance remains unchanged as months and years go by. As he descends into a life of debauchery and crime, the painting begins to take on a disfigured appearance that becomes grotesque as he commits one moral offense after another. Toward the end of the story, Dorian, still looking as young and handsome as ever, alternates between amused and horrified by the hideous reflection of his soul staring out from the painting. He begins to regret his wish and wonders if it is too late to make amends and redeem his soul. As one would expect, the story ends tragically, reminding us of the price one may unwittingly pay for vanity, hedonism, and selfish indulgence.

To understand how Oscar Wilde developed this story, and to fully appreciate its irony as a sort of auto-biographical window into his own sordid life and pursuit of decadent pleasure, we must go back in time and explore the details of his life.

Wilde achieved great success and fame as a nineteenth-century Irish playwright and poet. Known for wearing flamboyant fashions and making outrageous statements, he became one of the best-known literary celebrities of his time. Born Oscar Fingal O'Flahertie Wills Wilde on October 16, 1854, he was the son of Sir William Wilde, a prominent eye and ear surgeon, and Jane Francesca Elgee, a writer and Irish nationalist. Raised in Dublin, he was home-schooled through age nine, and he spoke fluent French and German, which he learned from the maids in his home. He attended Trinity College in Dublin, where he earned The Berkeley Gold Medal, the highest award for students of classical studies and literature. He went on to attend Magdalen College at Oxford, where he earned the coveted Sir Roger Newdigate Prize for his poem *Ravenna* in 1878 and graduated that fall with top honors in two fields of study.

Two of Wilde's tutors at Oxford introduced him to *aestheticism*, an emerging philosophy that emphasized the aesthetic value of art, or "art for art's sake," over sociopolitical themes in literature, music, and art. Wilde also embraced the Decadent movement, a late nineteenth-century literary and artistic philosophy that advocated excess and artificiality. These philosophies shocked Victorian Europe by challenging social norms at a time when many believed literature and art should reflect proper behavior and established social values; instead, they encouraged a revolution in thinking that favored artistic, political, and sexual experimentation and freedom.

Providing insight into the social and cultural trends that influenced Wilde's life and writings, Dr. Carolyn Burdett, a senior lecturer in Victorian Studies at the University of London, states in an article published on the British Library website: "Many Victorians passionately believed that literature and art fulfilled important ethical roles. Literature provided models of correct behavior: it allowed people to identify with situations in which good actions were rewarded, or it provoked tender emotions...The supporters of aestheticism, however, disagreed, arguing that art had nothing to do with morality. Instead, art was primarily about the elevation of taste and the pure pursuit of beauty. More controversially, the aesthetes also saw these qualities as guiding principles for life. They argued that the arts should be judged on form rather than morality. The famous motto 'art for art's sake' encapsulates this view."

After graduating from Magdalen College, Wilde returned to Dublin, where he fell in love with Florence Balcombe. When the young woman spurned his affection and instead became engaged to Bram Stoker, the author of *Dracula*, Wilde vowed to leave Ireland and never return. He spent the next six years on a lecture tour that took him to Paris, London, the United States, and Canada.

In 1884, Wilde married Constance Lloyd, the daughter of Horace Lloyd, the Queen's personal lawyer. Constance came from an affluent family and was given a substantial allowance that enabled her and her new husband to enjoy a life of luxury and ease. Soon, Wilde was hobnobbing with aristocrats and mingling in London's elite social circles. His keen wit, intellect, and flamboyant personality quickly elevated him to celebrity status.

Around 1890, Wilde turned his attention to writing essays. In 1891, he wrote his only novel, *The Picture of Dorian Gray,* in which he merged aestheticism, decadence, and beauty into a literary work that incited a firestorm of controversy. A year later, while visiting Paris, he wrote

Salome, a one-act play that recounts the Biblical story of Salome, stepdaughter of the first-century ruler Herod Antipas, who demands the head of John the Baptist on a silver platter as a reward for dancing the Dance of the Seven Veils. England refused to grant a performance license for the provocative play. Wilde went on to produce four acclaimed society comedies over the next few years, which made him one of the most popular late-Victorian playwrights in England.

Wilde was a Freemason for a time, before his membership lapsed for nonpayment of dues. He scorned "manly" sports, although he occasionally stepped into the boxing ring. He wore his hair long and loved peacock feathers, sunflowers, lilies, and blue china.

In February 1895, at the pinnacle of Wilde's success, and while *The Importance of Being Earnest* was being performed to critical acclaim in London, the Marquess of Queensberry became incensed over an alleged homosexual relationship between Wilde and his son, Alfred. Queensberry left a calling card at Wilde's club with the handwritten message: "For Oscar Wilde, posing as a Somdomite [sic]." The accusation was scandalous and carried serious legal ramifications: homosexuality was not only a social taboo in late nineteenth-century England—it was a criminal offense that could lead to imprisonment.

Wilde filed a lawsuit against Queensberry for criminal libel, which led to the aristocrat's arrest. London's social circles

John Douglas, 9th Marquess of Queensberry (1896)

were riveted by the unfolding controversy, fueled in part by widespread disdain for Queensberry, whose sordid background included messy divorces, charges of brutality, involvement in the then-disreputable sport of boxing, and being an outspoken atheist.

Tragically for Wilde, the lawsuit was a mistake that embroiled him in a vicious scandal and ultimately led to his downfall and a prison sentence. His friends had cautioned that suing Queensberry was a bad idea, and one friend urged Wilde to flee to France, predicting: "They are going to prove sodomy against you." He resented the advice and stormed out, complaining: "It is at such moments as these that one sees who are one's true friends."

At trial, Queensberry's lawyers portrayed Wilde as a vile older man who seduced young boys into a despicable life of homosexuality and crime. They presented evidence that he had paid a dozen young male prostitutes for sex. Under British law, the best defense against libel was to show that the contested statements were true. Faced with damning evidence, Wilde's lawyers realized that they could not win, and the lawsuit was dropped.

Queensberry countersued to recover his substantial costs of hiring lawyers and private detectives for his defense. Wilde lost and was forced into bankruptcy. His assets were seized and auctioned off, and Queensberry got further revenge when he reported Wilde's scandalous conduct to Scotland Yard. Acting on evidence that Wilde had solicited and sodomized twelve young boys over the course of two years, police arrested and charged him. He was convicted of gross indecency and sentenced to two years of hard labor.

Initially, Wilde was jailed at Newgate Prison in London and then moved to Pentonville, where he served his "hard labor" sentence by walking on a treadmill for many hours and performing backbreaking menial tasks. The only books available to read were *The Pilgrim's Progress* and the Bible. After a few months, Wilde was moved to Wandsworth Prison, where the continued regimen of hard labor caused his health to deteriorate. After he collapsed from illness and hunger, breaking an eardrum in the fall, he spent two months in the infirmary and was then transferred to Reading Gaol, west of London. While being transported, he sank to the low point in his life as a crowd shouted insults and spat on him at the railway station.

Wilde was released from prison in May 1897. Penniless, and his health ruined by the harsh conditions of his incarceration, he fled to France, where he lived in exile until he died in a Paris hotel at age 46.

Humiliated by the scandal that consumed London's social circles with sordid gossip, Wilde's wife, Constance, changed

Wilde's prison cell at Reading Gaol as it appears today.

her last name to Holland to escape the notoriety and protect her two sons that she'd had with Wilde: Cyril, who was killed on a French battlefield during World War I, and Vyvyan, who became an author and translator.

The publication of Oscar Wilde's only novel in 1890 was in some respects a harbinger of his own descent into a life of self-indulgence and debauchery. In fact, he once said that the three main characters of the story were reflections of himself: "Basil Hallward (the artist) is what I think I am: Lord Henry (the hedonist) is what the world thinks of me: Dorian is what I would like to be—in other ages, perhaps." The book's daring embrace of decadence and sexual themes sparked a furor at the time. Today, the work is regarded as a great classic, a suspenseful and thought-provoking masterpiece that is as disturbing as it is intriguing.

The Characters of the Story

Dorian Gray: The main character. An exceedingly handsome young man who views a painting of himself and wishes aloud that he could retain his youth and beauty, while the painting ages. His wish is granted, and Dorian submerges himself in a life of pleasure seeking and debauchery that has dire consequences.

Basil Hallward: An artist who paints Dorian's portrait, which he believes is his masterpiece. After Dorian reveals that the painting has changed into a horribly disfigured old man, he murders Basil in a fit of paranoid rage.

Lord Henry Wotton: A witty, sarcastic nobleman who enjoys impressing and influencing Dorian. He encourages Dorian to pursue a life of debauchery. A notorious philanderer, he once told Basil: "You seem to forget that I am married, and the one charm of marriage is that it makes a life of deception absolutely necessary for both parties."

Lady Victoria Wotton: Lord Henry's wife, who eventually tires of his frequent affairs and disdain, and she divorces him. Lord Henry describes her as hopelessly romantic, her efforts to look pretty only made her seem untidy, and "she had a perfect mania for going to church."

Sibyl Vane: A beautiful young actress from a poor family who performs Shakespearean plays at the local theatre. She is Dorian's first love. But when Dorian realizes that he was in love with the characters she played rather than Sibyl, he harshly renounces his love for her, and she commits suicide. Lord Henry likens her death to the fate of Ophelia in *Hamlet*.

James Vane: Sibyl's brother. A sailor who plans to sail to Australia. When Sibyl falls in love with Dorian, he nearly cancels his trip but ultimately sails and swears vengeance upon Dorian if any harm comes to his sister. After her suicide, James returns to Europe to kill Dorian, but he is accidentally shot by a hunter.

Mrs. Vane: Sibyl's mother, she is older, single, and poor. She likes Dorian for his wealth and, hoping that his affluence would rub off on her family, she encourages her daughter's involvement with "Prince Charming."

Lady Agatha: Lord Henry's aunt, who is active in charity work in London. She hosts a luncheon attended by Henry and Dorian Gray.

Lord Fermor (Uncle George): Lord Henry's uncle. He tells his nephew the story of Dorian Gray's sordid family history.

Lady Brandon: She introduces Basil to Dorian Gray at a party.

Alan Campbell: A chemist, musician, and Dorian's former friend who severed the relationship when Dorian's pursuit of pleasure took a sinister turn. Later, Dorian blackmails him into helping dispose of Basil Hallward's body after he murdered the painter in a paranoid rage. Campbell assists in the nefarious deed but kills himself afterward.

Sir Geoffrey Clouston: The Duchess of Monmouth's brother. He shoots and kills James Vane in a freak hunting accident

Margaret Devereux: Dorian's deceased mother, mentioned by Lord Fermor.

Adrian Singleton: A young man who befriends Dorian and ends up addicted to opium, estranged from his family, and his reputation and life ruined.

Duchess of Monmouth (Gladys): A pretty, young socialite. She is married to an older nobleman, bored, and flirts with Dorian.

Victor: Dorian's first servant. Though a faithful employee, he provoked Dorian's suspicions, and he was let go. They parted company amicably.

Francis: Dorian's servant who replaces Victor.

Lady Gwendolyn: Lord Henry's sister. She has a scandalous affair with Dorian.

Hansom Driver: An unnamed man who drives Dorian to the local opium den.

Mr. Hubbard: A frame maker. Dorian asks for the man's help with concealing his portrait in the attic of his home. Hubbard and his assistant agree to lend a hand.

Mr. Isaacs: The manager of the theater where Sibyl Vane performed, and where she met Dorian Gray and fell in love.

Lord Kelso: Dorian's hardhearted grandfather who raised Dorian after the death of his parents, Kelso apparently had his own daughter's husband killed.

Parker: Basil Hallward's butler.

Thornton: The gamekeeper at the hunt in Chapter 18. He delivers startling news about the stranger who had been accidentally shot while hiding in a bush.

Woman at Bar: One of Dorian's early victims who claims he ruined her life. When she encounters James Vane at the bar of an opium den, she identifies Dorian.

Mrs. Leaf: Dorian's housekeeper. A no-nonsense, older woman who performs her job efficiently. She gives the keys to the attic room to Dorian.

Lady Narborough: An aging widow of a wealthy aristocrat, she married off her daughters to rich, elderly men and now devotes herself to a life of leisure. She hosts a dinner party attended by Dorian and Lord Henry in Chapter 15.

Hetty Merton: A beautiful but naïve village girl who reminds Dorian of Sibyl Vane. He resists the temptation to corrupt her and is proud of his self-restraint, hoping that his act of kindness might help redeem his soul.

Chapter 1 Review

Basil Hallward is an artist working on his latest portrait. His friend, Lord Henry Wotton, asks him about the masterpiece he is creating and suggests that he display it at a local gallery. Basil says he probably won't display it because he has "put too much of himself into it." Lord Henry presses Basil for details about the subject of his painting—an exquisitely handsome young man named Dorian Gray. Basil is clearly quite fond of Dorian and refers to him as his muse and sole inspiration. When a servant enters to announce Dorian's arrival, Lord Henry insists on meeting him. Basil frets about this and requests that he not influence or "spoil" Dorian in any way.

Discussion Topics:

1. Why does Basil refer to Dorian as "a dream of form in days of thought"?

2. Identify the speaker and explain this quotation: "How pleasant it was in the garden! And how delightful other people's emotions were!—much more delightful than their ideas, it seemed to him."

3. What do you think Basil means when he says that he "put too much of himself" into his portrait of Dorian Gray?

4. What does Lord Henry's views on marriage expressed in Chapter 1 reveal about his character and lifestyle?

Chapter Quiz:

1.01: What does Basil request of Lord Henry before he introduces him to Dorian Gray?
a) He asks Lord Henry to urge Dorian to have his portrait painted.
b) He asks Lord Henry not to influence Dorian.
c) He urges Lord Henry to leave without meeting Dorian.
d) He asks Lord Henry not to mention the painting to Dorian.

1.02: Who is Basil Hallward?
a) the mayor of Dorian's hometown
b) a wandering gypsy
c) the brother of a girl Dorian dates
d) a well-known artist

1.03: What do Lord Basil and Lord Henry discuss in this chapter?
a) a loan Basil requests to help pay the rent on his art studio
b) the subject of a beautiful painting created by Hallward
c) Lord Henry's marital problems
d) their differing views on politics and religion

1.04: Why does Basil not want to exhibit his portrait of Dorian Gray?
a) Basil believes he has put too much of himself into the painting.
b) to protect Dorian's privacy
c) He believes the painting is not good enough to exhibit.
d) Basil feels the painting is just a quick sketch and nothing special.

1.05: How does Basil initially meet Dorian?
a) through a newspaper advertisement for models
b) while admiring a famous painting in a local museum
c) in Basil's art studio
d) at a party hosted by Lady Brandon

1.06: Dorian became an obsession for Basil, who declared that he was...
a) his long-lost brother
b) his sole inspiration
c) a strange but powerful mentor

1.07: Basil sensed that despite his beauty, Dorian was on the verge of a terrible crisis.
a) True
b) False

1.08: In what location does the novel begin?
a) Lord Henry's mansion
b) a local tavern on the outskirts of town
c) Basil Hallward's home
d) outside a Catholic church

1.09: Dorian Gray's hair color is described as...
a) silver
b) jet black
c) golden
d) His hair color isn't mentioned.

Chapter 2 Review

Dorian enters the studio, and Basil introduces him to Lord Henry, who engages the young man in thoughtful conversation while Basil puts the finishing touches on his painting. Henry shares his life philosophies with Dorian and remarks that his youth and beauty are magnificent things, but he warns that those qualities will fade quickly. He advises Dorian to live his life to the fullest, embrace pleasure, and always seek new sensations. When Basil finishes the painting, Dorian gazes at it sadly. Thinking about Lord Henry's remarks, he reflects on the fact that the painting will remain forever young while he himself will grow old and decrepit, and he wishes that it were the other way around.

Discussion Topics:

1. Why is Dorian sad when he views his finished portrait?

2. What is Lord Henry's view on the morality of influencing others?

3. What influence does Lord Henry's words have on Dorian?

4. Identify the speaker and explain the passage: "And beauty is a form of genius —is higher, indeed, than genius, as it needs no explanation."

Chapter Quiz:

2.01: Which one of the following statements is correct?
a) Lord Henry warned Basil that Dorian might steal money from him.
b) Dorian warned Basil that Lord Henry was insanely jealous.
c) Basil warned Dorian that Lord Henry is a bad influence.
d) None of these statements are correct.

2.02: What is Lord Henry's personal philosophy?
a) Live for the moment and cherish happy memories.
b) The highest of all duties is the duty that one owes to one's self.
c) Live free or die.
d) The rich get richer, the poor get poorer.

2.03: Lord Henry warned Dorian that...
a) Dorian's youth and beauty will quickly fade.
b) Dorian will be cursed if Basil paints his portrait.
c) Basil possesses supernatural powers.

2.04: Basil urged Dorian to live life to its fullest and devote himself to seeking new sensations rather than pursuing common pastimes.
a) True
b) False

2.05: How did Lord Henry feel about Basil's finished portrait of Dorian?
a) It frightened him—he sensed something evil about the painting.
b) He said that the portrait didn't resemble Dorian at all.
c) He liked the colors, but thought the pose should have been different.
d) He called it the finest thing of modern times.

2.06: Why was Dorian unhappy when he saw his finished portrait?
a) He thought that Basil made him look ugly.
b) He thought that Basil made him look better than he really looked.
c) He lamented that the portrait would remain forever young, while he grows old.
d) He felt cheated because Basil should have paid him to sit as a model.

2.07: What did Basil decide to do with the finished painting?
a) He gave it to Dorian Gray as a gift.
b) He burned the painting.
c) He displayed it in the local museum.
d) He gave the painting to Lord Henry.

2.08: What stuns Dorian when he initially meets Lord Henry?
a) what Lord Henry says about Dorian's beauty
b) what Lord Henry says about Basil's painting
c) what Lord Henry says about youth
d) Lord Henry curses at Basil in an angry rage.

Chapter 3 Review

Lord Henry visits his uncle, Lord Fermor, and asks about Dorian Gray's past. Fermor recounts that Dorian's mother was a beautiful noblewoman who eloped with a poor soldier. Her father arranged to have her husband killed before Dorian was born, and Dorian's mother died not long after. Learning of Dorian's scandalous past fascinates Lord Henry even further. At a dinner party with his aunt, politicians, and local aristocrats, the guests delight in his charm, despite his vulgarity.

Discussion Topics:

1. Explain Lord Henry's definition of a paradox? How does this definition foreshadow events in the story?

2. Lord Henry tells Dorian: "All I want to do now is to look at life." What can we learn by observing life? How does this remark apply to the story?

3. Discuss how Lord Henry views conventional morality and how he challenges it. What does he say about resisting temptation?

4. What does Lord Henry reveal about his character when he says that history would have been different if cavemen knew how to laugh?

Chapter Quiz:

3.01: Who is Lord Henry's uncle?
a) Basil
b) Lord Fermor
c) King George
d) Lord Femur

3.02: What do Lord Henry and his uncle talk about in Chapter 3?
a) the state of politics in England
b) the British monarchy
c) Dorian Gray's past

3.03: What happened to Dorian Gray's father?
a) He killed Dorian's mother and was sent to prison.
b) He was killed in a freak weather accident.
c) The reader never learns what happened to Dorian's father.
d) He was killed just before Dorian was born.

3.04: What happened to Dorian Gray's mother?
a) She died soon after his birth.
b) She caught the flu when Dorian was four and died.
c) She died of the plague.
d) She ran off to France, and Dorian never heard from her again.

3.05: Who raised Dorian Gray?
a) his aunt
b) a half-sister from his father's previous marriage
c) a loveless tyrant
d) Lord Henry raised Dorian.

3.06: How does Lord Henry react when he learns about Dorian's unfortunate past?
a) He becomes increasingly fascinated with Dorian.
b) He grows despondent and refuses to speak with Dorian again.
c) He urges Dorian to get psychiatric help.
d) He orders Dorian to stay away from Lord Henry's young child.

3.07: Who is Lord Henry's aunt?
a) Queen Elizabeth
b) Lady Agatha
c) Lady Margaret
d) Princess Diana

3.08: What does Lord Henry speak about that shocks the group of socialites at lunch?
a) Darwin's theory of evolution
b) the virtues of hedonism and selfishness
c) He confesses that he killed his own brother.
d) the reasons why he believes in creationism

3.09: Despite feeling appalled by Lord Henry, how do the socialite guests view him?
a) They fear him because he is powerful and corrupt.
b) The guests abhor having to be in the same room with him.
c) They secretly view him with pity because he is a lost and bitter man.
d) The guests feel he is clever, charming, and fascinating.

Chapter 4 Review

Dorian meets Lord Henry's wife, Lady Victoria, who recognizes Dorian from the many photos her husband has of him. The two discuss music, and when Dorian echoes one of her husband's opinions, Victoria remarks that she often hears his opinions repeated by his friends. After Henry enters and Victoria leaves, Dorian shares news of his newfound love, Sibyl Vane, saying he wants Henry and Basil to meet her. When Henry arrives home that night, he finds a telegram from Dorian announcing his engagement to marry Sibyl.

Discussion Topics:

1. Describe Lord Henry's philosophy on women and relationships.

2. Explain why Sibyl Vane is an important character in the story.

3. What attracts Dorian to Sibyl?

4. Identify the speaker and explain the passage: "Men marry because they are tired; women, because they are curious: both are disappointed."

Chapter Quiz:

4.01: How many pictures did Lady Henry claim her husband had of Dorian?

a) only the one portrait that Basil painted

b) 17, maybe 18

c) more than 25

d) more than 100

4.02: What was Lord Henry's belief about time?

a) Punctuality is the thief of time, and he is always late.

b) Time waits for no one.

c) Time is money.

d) Lost time is never found again.

4.03: How did Dorian describe Lady Henry's dresses?

a) They fit her curves quite nicely.

b) Dorian was shocked that a wealthy noblewoman dressed so frumpy.

c) They looked as if they had been designed in a rage and put on in a tempest.

4.04: What did Lord Henry tell Dorian about marriage?
a) Never marry.
b) Men marry because they are tired, women because they are curious.
c) Those who do marry end up disappointed.
d) All of these answers are correct.

4.05: What news does Dorian share with Lord Henry in this chapter?
a) He confesses that he killed his best friend.
b) He tells him that he is in love.
c) He tells Lord Henry that he inherited a vast sum of money.
d) He reveals that he has seen a vision of the future.

4.06: Who is Dorian in love with?
a) Sibyl Vane
b) Lady Henry
c) Lord Basil
d) His father's stepdaughter

4.07: What is Henry's response when Dorian claims Sibyl is a genius?
a) No woman is a genius.
b) Women are a decorative gender.
c) Women never have anything to say, but they say it charmingly.

4.08: What is Sibyl Vane's occupation?
a) piano player
b) prostitute
c) schoolteacher
d) actress

4.09: How long has Dorian known Sibyl at this point in the story?
a) four months
b) about one year
c) about three weeks

4.10: What play did Sibyl perform the night Dorian initially met her?
a) Romeo and Juliet
b) Hamlet
c) Midsummer Night's Dream
d) The Raven

4.11: When did Dorian speak to Sibyl for the first time?
a) on the first night
b) on the third night
c) two weeks later
d) over a month later

4.12: How did Lord Henry describe Basil's personality?
a) Basil puts all that is charming about himself into his work, so he has nothing left for life but prejudices, principles, and common sense.
b) Basil is a fool, but highly creative, probably a genius, but he has no common sense.
c) Basil will always be a poor, struggling artist because he cannot manage or save money.

4.13: How often does Dorian go to watch Sibyl perform?
a) He goes every night.
b) He saw her perform only once.
c) He attended on her opening night and closing night.
d) He never actually saw her perform.

4.14: When Lord Henry arrived home about half-past midnight, he saw a telegram lying on the hall table from Dorian. What did it say?
a) Dorian announced his engagement to marry Sibyl Vane.
b) Dorian had killed someone and needed Lord Henry's help.
c) Dorian was stranded in London and needed money to return home.
d) The telegram contained two cryptic words: "I'm done."

Chapter 5 Review

Sibyl talks to her mother about her romance with Dorian. Her mother says she must focus on her acting, but if Dorian is rich, it may be a good thing. Sibyl's brother, James, arrives. We learn that he is a sailor and soon to depart for Australia. He and Sibyl go for a walk, and she suggests that many fantastic adventures await her brother in Australia. James is very protective of her and asks about her new friend. He worries about Dorian's intentions. A conversation between James and his mother at the end of the chapter reveals that she never married his father, although she insists that they were in love. This causes James more alarm, as he worries that his mother will let Sibyl follow in her footsteps.

Discussion Topics:

1. What does James Vane promise his sister?

2. What is Sibyl's nickname for Dorian?

3. How does Sibyl's mother feel about Dorian?

4. What does the conversation about Dorian between Sibyl's brother and her mother reveal?

Chapter Quiz:

5.01: What did Sibyl talk about on her walk with James?
a) She predicted that he would find great love and riches in Australia.
b) She feared that she would never see him again.
c) She feared that both of their parents would die while James away.
d) She angrily vowed that she would never say his name again.

5.02: How much money did the Vane family owe to Mr. Isaacs?
a) 50 pounds
b) 100 pounds
c) 500 quid
d) 2,000 pounds

5.03: Who is James Vane to Sibyl?
a) her father
b) her brother
c) her uncle
d) her stepbrother

5.04: What did Sibyl's mother say about happiness?

a) She had never been happy once in her life and she hoped her daughter would fare better.

b) Marriage is the cause of all unhappiness, so don't ever marry.

c) She was only happy when she saw her daughter act, and Sibyl should think of nothing other than acting.

d) None of these answers are correct.

5.05: Where is James Vane planning to travel?

a) France

b) Egypt

c) Australia

d) Germany

5.06: Why was James leery about taking Sibyl to walk in the park?

a) He was too shabby; only swell people walk in the park.

b) He was afraid they would both be mugged.

c) He felt that her dress was too revealing and would attract negative attention to her.

d) He worried that he would run into a drug dealer from his past.

5.07: Why is James worried about leaving for Australia?

a) He fears that he may catch malaria and die.

b) He doesn't believe his mother will watch over Sibyl properly.

c) He worries that his parents will pass away before he returns to visit.

d) He fears that he will run out of money once there.

5.08: What does James question his mother about in this chapter?

a) his father's failing health

b) his mother's rumored affair with Lord Henry

c) her finances and what she will leave for his inheritance

d) rumors about a mysterious man who comes to watch his sister perform every night

5.09: How was the sight of James and Sibyl walking together described?

a) He was a gallant young man walking with a princess.

b) He was like a common gardener walking with a rose.

c) He walked one step behind her because he was poorly dressed.

d) He walked one step in front of her because she was poorly dressed.

5.10: Which sibling is older: Sibyl or James?
a) James is younger than Sibyl.
b) James is older than Sibyl.
c) James and Sibyl are twins and thus the same age.
d) It is not revealed in the book which of the two is older.

5.11: How old is James in this chapter?
a) 12
b) 16
c) 18
d) 22

5.12: What was James brooding about during his walk with Sibyl?
a) the notion that his parents might die while he was in Australia, and he would be deprived of his inheritance
b) the fear of going to a strange land where he knew no one
c) the mysterious suiter courting his sister and their mother's inability to protect her
d) All of these answers are correct.

5.13: After walking with Sibyl in the park, what question did James ask their mother over dinner?
a) Did his mother love his father, and was she faithful to him?
b) Was his mother ever married to his father?
c) Was Sibyl born out of wedlock?
d) Did his mother ever have an illicit affair?

Chapter 6 Review

Lord Henry meets with Basil and tells him of Dorian's engagement. They discuss Sibyl and agree that it is a foolish decision for him to marry so far beneath him. Dorian joins them and says he proposed, but it was more inferred because he did not speak the words directly, claiming it wasn't necessary, as they are in love and had an understanding. The three men discuss their views on the nature of pleasure and then go to the theater to watch Sibyl perform. Basil makes the trip alone while reflecting upon his sadness over Dorian's decision to marry.

Discussion Topics:

1. What news does Lord Henry share with Basil early in this chapter?

2. Does Sibyl have any influence on Dorian? Give an example.

3. What does Dorian's description of Sibyl playing Rosalind suggest about his sexual preferences?

Chapter Quiz:

6.01: What news did Lord Henry share with Basil at dinner?
a) Dorian Gray was engaged to be married.
b) A friend of Lord Henry's wanted Basil to paint a portrait of his wife.
c) Dorian Gray had killed a man who threatened Sibyl Vane.
d) None of these answers are correct.

6.02: Why did Basil think that Dorian's engagement was absurd?
a) He believed Sibyl was too young and immature for Dorian.
b) He felt that Dorian would never find happiness in marriage.
c) He was convinced that Sibyl would be unfaithful and hurt Dorian.
d) He believed Dorian should not marry someone so beneath him.

6.03: Why does Lord Henry say that being unselfish is a bad thing?
a) Unselfish people squander their time and money on less fortunate people who don't deserve their generosity.
b) Unselfish people will never have wealth because they give all their money away.
c) Unselfish people are boring and lack individuality.
d) Unselfish people turn into martyrs and destroy themselves.

6.04: What did Lord Henry expect would happen with Dorian and Sibyl?

a) Dorian would marry Sibyl for six months and become infatuated with someone else.

b) Dorian would come to his senses and cancel the wedding.

c) Sibyl would have a tragic accident soon after the marriage.

d) Dorian and Sibyl would marry and live happily ever after.

6.05: Basil appeals to Dorian because he represents all the sins that Dorian has never had the courage to commit.

a) True

b) False

Chapter 7 Review

The theater where Sibyl performs is crowded, hot, and dirty. When Lord Henry and Basil see Sibyl, they agree that she is beautiful but her acting is terrible. They leave after the second act because Henry can no longer bear watching her. Dorian angrily confronts Sibyl after the play, and she explains that acting no longer interests her because she found true love, which was more blissful than any emotion or character she could ever act out. Dorian replies that she has ruined their love, and she means nothing to him now. He leaves her weeping on the floor. That night when he arrives home, he notices that his likeness in Basil's portrait has developed lines and a cruelness to the mouth. Intrigued, he recalls his wish that the painting rather than himself should reflect the mark of his age and lifestyle. Ashamed at his behavior, he covers the painting and goes to bed, determined to make amends to Sibyl in the morning.

Discussion Topics:

1. Describe in your own words the theater where Sibyl performs.

2. How do Lord Henry and Basil feel about Sibyl and her performance?

3. How does Sibyl explain her mediocre performance to Dorian, and how does he react to her explanation?

4. How does the author build suspense before revealing that Dorian's portrait has changed?

Chapter Quiz:

7.01: What is the temperature in the theater on the night recounted in this chapter?

a) It was bone-numbingly cold.
b) It was very hot.
c) The temperature was quite comfortable.
d) The temperature in the theater is not mentioned.

7.02: What did Basil and Lord Henry think of Sibyl when they saw her perform?

a) She was a wonderful actress and played her role well.
b) She was neither pretty nor talented.
c) She was quite beautiful, but she couldn't act.
d) They were certain that she would be famous one day.

7.03: After Sibyl's performance, Dorian complained: "Last night she was a great artist. This evening, she is merely a commonplace mediocre actress."
a) True
b) False

7.04: What happened in this chapter after the second act of the play?
a) Sibyl lost her balance and fell off the stage.
b) Dorian and Lord Henry argued because the latter criticized Sibyl's performance.
c) Lord Henry and Basil left early because they could not bear to watch Sibyl's mediocre performance any longer.
d) All of these answers are correct.

7.05: When Sibyl announced that her acting career was over, Dorian realized that he was in love with her talent and with the characters she played, not with Sibyl herself.
a) True
b) False

7.06: How did Dorian respond to Sibyl saying her acting career was over?
a) He was silent and kept his thoughts to himself.
b) He was gentle and tried his best to console her.
c) He was embarrassed, disappointed, and upset: "You have killed my love," he declared.
d) He only pretended to be kind and forced himself to act consoling.

7.07: How did Sibyl respond to Dorian's anger?
a) She slapped him in the face and then broke into tears.
b) She listened, with a hurt look in her eyes, but said nothing.
c) She cried and threw herself at his feet, begging him not to leave her.
d) She cursed at him and said she never wanted to see him again.

7.08: How did Dorian feel about Sibyl's tears?
a) He felt nothing and did not react.
b) Her tears made him feel sad and guilty.
c) Her tears annoyed him.
d) None of these answers are correct.

7.09: What was Sibyl's explanation for her bad acting?

a) She felt weak and dizzy, and feared she was coming down the flu.

b) She thought she had given a great performance, and she was hurt by Dorian's contempt.

c) After she saw Dorian flirting with another woman at the theater, she was consumed by jealousy and forget her lines.

d) Her characters and their emotions no longer interested her because she had fallen in love.

7.10: After Dorian expressed dismay over Sibyl's performance, what did he notice about the painting when he returned home that night?

a) The colors in the portrait were brighter and more vibrant.

b) The expression in the painting seemed different; there was a touch of cruelty to the mouth.

c) His image seemed to be a year or two younger.

d) He didn't notice anything different.

7.11: After reflecting on his harsh treatment of Sibyl, what did Dorian decide to do?

a) Stop listening to Lord Henry's poisonous theories and try to make amends to Sibyl

b) Provoke another argument with Sibyl to make her despise him

c) Ask Lord Henry for advice

d) Live a sinful, hedonistic existence with no regrets

7.12: How did Lord Henry compare art to love?

a) Art and love mirror life.

b) Art inspires love, and love inspires art.

c) Without love, there can be no art.

d) Art and love are simply forms of imitation.

Chapter 8 Review

Dorian awakens after an extended sleep. He checks the painting to see if the changes he saw last night were real or imagined. He frets that the face in the portrait has indeed changed and seems even more cruel than it was the night before. His servant brings him breakfast and a pile of letters, including one from Lord Henry that was hand-delivered in the morning. Dorian ignores the stack of mail and instead writes his own letter, an apologetic and passionate ode to Sibyl. Henry arrives and insists on seeing Dorian, who is shocked when he learns of Sibyl's death. After going through a series of emotions while talking to Henry, he decides that this incident is a turning point in his life and he will now accept his destiny of "eternal youth, infinite passion, pleasures subtle and secret, wild joy, and wilder sins." That evening he joins Lord Henry at the Opera.

Discussion Topics:

1. Explain the uncanny power of Dorian's portrait in one sentence.

2. When Dorian realizes what is happening to the painting, what does he do with it?

3. Explain why Lord Henry compared Sibyl to Shakespeare's characters Desdemona, Ophelia, and Juliet.

Chapter Quiz:

8.01: The day after Dorian's harsh reaction to Sibyl's performance, what time did he awaken?

a) as the sun was coming up

b) well past noon

c) 9 a.m.

d) 11 a.m.

8.02: When Dorian awoke, what did he see when he examined Basil's painting?

a) It looked the same as it did on the day Basil finished it.

b) His portrait had changed, and the expression seemed even more cruel than it was the night before.

c) The painting had a strange, iridescent glow.

d) His image in the painting was at least five years younger.

8.03: After much reflection on the painting, to whom did Dorian write a letter?
a) Lord Henry
b) Basil
c) Sibyl

8.04: Who knocked at the door as Dorian finished writing a letter?
a) Lord Henry
b) Sibyl
c) Basil
d) Sibyl's mother

8.05: When Dorian told Lord Henry that he had caused a dreadful scene with Sibyl the night before, but he was determined to make amends and marry her, Henry laughed and said Dorian was too worried about things which would be of little consequence when he looks back over his life.
a) True
b) False

8.06: What did Dorian think of Lord Henry's advice on life, relationships, and his ill-fated romance with Sibyl after her death?
a) He felt repulsed by Lord Henry's cavalier attitude and wondered what terrible life experiences had made him that way.
b) He felt relief and thanked Lord Henry for being his best friend.
c) He decided to ignore Lord Henry's advice and promised himself that he would work to become a better person.
d) None of these answers are correct.

8.07: After Sibyl's death, who convinces Dorian to avoid becoming involved in the investigation?
a) Basil
b) Sibyl's mother
c) Lady Henry
d) Lord Henry

8.08: Lord Henry was concerned about Sibyl's death because he feared that an inquest might be held, and it would be unwise for Basil and his painting to be mixed up in a scandal.
a) True
b) False

8.09: How did Sibyl die?

a) She killed herself by jumping off a high cliff near her home.

b) She fell from her horse while riding alone and died tragically.

c) She was found dead on the floor of her dressing room at the theater after ingesting a poisonous substance.

d) She went for a late-night walk in a local park and was strangled by an unknown assailant.

8.10: Why did Lord Henry advise Dorian not to waste tears over Sibyl?

a) She was less real than the characters she played in her acting.

b) She was a commoner, beneath Dorian's position and wealth, and she would have brought him nothing but heartache.

c) He assured Dorian that his one true love was still out there, and one day they would meet.

d) Love, he said, is ridiculous, and humans should learn to never feel this emotion.

Chapter 9 Review

Basil visits Dorian to offer condolences about Sibyl's death. Dorian says that her death belongs in the past: "What is done is done. What is past is past." Basil feels anger towards Lord Henry for having such a strong influence on Dorian, and he asks Dorian to sit for another painting. Dorian refuses, saying he will never sit for Basil again. He demands that Basil tell him his secret of why he didn't want to display the painting in a museum.

As the chapter unfolds, Basil confesses that he had painted Dorian many times, as mythical and historic characters, and he was obsessed with him. Dorian can't imagine ever being influenced by someone as deeply as Basil was by him, and he repeats that he won't sit for Basil again, and that they are merely friends.

Discussion Topics:

1. How does Basil react to Dorian's personality changes?
2. What are Basil's reasons for not exhibiting his portrait of Dorian?
3. Explain the passion of creation discussed in this chapter.
4. Why is Basil surprised by Dorian's behavior?
5. Why does Oscar Wilde invoke the words of French poet Gautier?

Chapter Quiz:

9.01: What did Dorian say about emotion?
a) Emotion is a waste of energy; it's better to feel nothing.
b) He did not want to be at the mercy of emotions; he wanted to use, enjoy, and dominate them.
c) You can't allow yourself the luxury of emotion if your goal is the pursuit of pleasure.
d) Only experience positive emotions; never fall prey to negativity.

9.02: What upset Basil about Dorian's reaction to Sibyl's death was that Lord Henry had exerted such a strong influence over someone who used to be so simple, natural, and affectionate.
a) True
b) False

9.03: Did Dorian get caught up in the investigation of Sibyl's death?
a) Yes, he did.
b) No, Sibyl did not even know Dorian's real name.
c) Dorian took the initiative and went to the inquest on his own.
d) The story doesn't reveal whether he is caught up in the inquest.

9.04: Dorian asked Basil to paint a portrait of...
a) Lord Henry
b) Dorian's mother
c) Sibyl
d) Dorian's father

9.05: Basil declared that he would never paint another portrait of Dorian, even though Dorian was eager to sit for him again.
a) True
b) False

9.06: How did Dorian respond to Basil's request to sit for him again?
a) He was flattered and promised he would make time to do it.
b) He was ambivalent and told Basil be would think about it.
c) He agreed but asked Basil to create a black and white ink drawing.
d) He refused, saying that he could never sit for Basil again.

9.07: When Dorian asked Basil why he had refused to exhibit his portrait, Basil answered:
a) "To be perfectly honest, it's none of your business, my friend."
b) "Dorian, if I told you, you might like me less than you do, and you would certainly laugh at me. "
c) "It is a paltry example of my skill as an artist, and I do not want to lose your respect or friendship."

9.08: What secret did Basil reveal to Dorian in this chapter?
a) He had drawn Dorian in many settings and created his most beautiful portrait ever. But because of his emotion and the realism of the method, he had put too much of himself into the painting.
b) Lord Henry was infatuated with him and had plotted to kidnap him.
c) He told Dorian that Sibyl's brother, James, had said that Sibyl was only attracted to Dorian for his wealth.
d) Basil never made any of these statements to Dorian.

Chapter 10 Review

Dorian asks his housekeeper for the key to the attic schoolroom so that he could move Basil's painting out of sight and lock it up. A frame-maker and his helper stop by the house and carry the painting upstairs. Dorian frets about anyone seeing it and is paranoid at the thought of anyone knowing where it is stored.

Once the painting is locked away, he sits down for tea and begins to read a yellow book sent to him by Lord Henry. Entranced, he concludes that the work is a "poisonous book" which confuses the boundaries of vice and virtue. He meets with Lord Henry later that night and tells him the book is fascinating.

Discussion Topics:

1. What is the yellow book? What does it come to represent for Dorian as the story unfolds?

2. Do you think it's too late for Dorian to redeem himself? Explain your reasoning.

3. Identify the speaker and explain the quote: "There were times when it appeared to Dorian Gray that the whole of history was merely the record of his own life, not as he had lived it in act and circumstance, but as his imagination had created it for him."

Chapter Quiz:

10.01: What did Dorian ask the housekeeper, Mrs. Leaf, to fetch for him?
a) the key to the old, attic schoolroom
b) the letter that Sibyl had written before she took her life
c) Basil's painting of Dorian
d) a bottle of wine

10.02: What was name of the servant with whom Dorian conversed in the first paragraph of this chapter?
a) Harry
b) Isabel
c) Victoria
d) Victor

10.03: What task did Mr. Hubbard and his assistant help Dorian with?
a) They helped him burn Basil's painting.
b) They carried the painting upstairs into the attic schoolroom.
c) They gave Dorian an alibi so he could avoid becoming entangled in Sibyl's inquest.
d) All of these answers are correct.

10.04: What did Dorian find with his tray of tea in the evening?
a) a newspaper, a letter from Lord Henry, and a key to the old schoolroom
b) a yellow book, a newspaper, and a letter from Lord Henry
c) Dorian's diary, a newspaper, and Sibyl's suicide note
d) an official order to appear at Sibyl's inquest

10.05: As Dorian looked over the newspaper in this chapter, what passage did he find circled in red ink?
a) an announcement of a social event at the local art gallery
b) an advertisement seeking portrait models, placed by Basil
c) a scandalous article about Lady Henry having a scandalous affair
d) an article about the inquest into Sibyl Vane's death

10.06: Why was Dorian late to meet Lord Henry?
a) He fell asleep while reading the newspaper.
b) He thought it was important to be fashionably late and keep Lord Henry waiting.
c) He lost track of time after becoming absorbed in the yellow book.
d) He was engrossed in conversation with his housekeeper, Mrs. Leaf.

10.07: Why did Dorian feel brief remorse that he had not confided to Basil the reason that he wanted to hide the portrait?
a) He knew Basil's love for him was noble and intellectual, and the artist would have helped him resist Lord Henry's influence and the more poisonous influences that came from his own temperament.
b) He knew that if he told Basil about the painting, the artist would have burned it and freed Dorian from its foul magic.
c) He wanted to confess to Basil how happy he was to be free to follow a life of depravity without suffering the consequences.
d) He was angry at Basil for painting the portrait and wanted the artist to know that his art had destroyed Dorian's life.

10.08: Which description fits Mr. Hubbard, the frame-maker of South Audley Street?
a) a very large man with a bushy white beard
b) an old man, hunched over, with dark eyes and a wise gaze
c) a florid, red-whiskered little man
d) a young man in his thirties, handsome, strapping, with the air of a celebrity or aristocrat

10.09: When Dorian decides that no one other than himself will ever see his portrait again, what does he do with the painting?
a) He hides it in the old schoolroom in his house.
b) He asks Mr. Hubbard, the frame-maker, to remove it from his house.
c) He orders his servants to help him burn the painting.
d) He donates the portrait to the local museum.

10.10: What gift from Lord Henry has a profound influence on Dorian?
a) a ring
b) a mirror
c) a book
d) a statue

Chapter 11 Review

This chapter spans Dorian's life as he ages through his twenties and thirties. He becomes obsessed with the yellow book from Lord Henry. He buys several copies and has them bound in various colors to suit his moods. As years go by, he develops a wide variety of interests and collects luxurious items for his home. He travels often, sometimes leaving mysteriously with no explanation. The locals begin to gossip, and his reputation suffers. He soon stops his travel fearing that someone will see his portrait while he is away. Throughout these years, he continues to read the yellow book and believes that it has poisoned his thinking.

Discussion Topics:

1. Why is Dorian unable to break free from the yellow books' influence?

2. Why is Basil Hallward leaving England?

3. When Basil says that locals are gossiping about him, how does Dorian react?

4. What tension between faith and intellect is brought to light through Dorian's attitudes on religion?

Chapter Quiz:

11.01: What did Dorian often do when he returned from his mysterious absences?
a) He went to the graveyard to mourn Sibyl.
b) He ordered his servants to lock him away in his room to keep him out of trouble.
c) He meditated in hopes that he would become a better person.
d) He went up to the schoolroom and stood with a mirror in front of his portrait.

11.02: What did Dorian do once or twice a month in the winter and on Wednesday's throughout the season?
a) He held dinner parties featuring celebrated musicians in his home.
b) He hosted a re-enactment of Romeo & Juliet to honor Sibyl's memory.
c) He went to the theater in search of young actresses whom he could beguile and seduce.
d) He visited Sibyl's mother and had dinner with her.

11.03: What interests did Dorian pursue in the years after Sibyl's death?
a) Catholicism, Darwinism, perfumes, music, and building collections of items with historical significance.
b) Zen, reincarnation, history, and coin collecting
c) travel and fine cuisine
d) history, geography, math, and medical science

11.04: Why did Dorian have so many collections of great treasures?
a) He sought greater wealth so he could avoid falling into poverty.
b) The beautiful items in his home afforded him an escape from the degradation of his life.
c) Realizing that he would never age made him become a hoarder.
d) He wanted more riches than anyone else in his community possessed.

11.05: How did Dorian feel as he often sat in front of the portrait?
a) He felt loathing, but also pride in his individualism.
b) He was saddened and wished that he had never met Basil.
c) He was thrilled about the prospect that he would never grow old.
d) He felt rage toward Basil because his painting had ruined his life.

11.06: Dorian curtailed his travels because he was fearful that someone might discover Basil's painting while he was away from home.
a) True
b) False

11.07: What happened to Dorian's reputation because of his travels and disappearances?
a) He became more popular as others noticed that he had somehow discovered the secret of eternal youth.
b) He grew paranoid and increasingly reluctant to leave his home for fear of being attacked.
c) He became the object of gossip and mistrust.
d) Journalists began speculating about him in the major newspapers.

11.08: How did Dorian feel about the gossip swirling around him?
a) He became fearful of going out in public and became more reclusive.
b) He plotted to murder Basil for creating a painting with supernatural powers that ruined his life.
c) He was unphased and felt that while gossip hurt him in the eyes of some, it raised his status to others.

11.09: The yellow book that Dorian received from Lord Henry made him view evil simply as a mode through which he could realize his conception of the beautiful.
a) True
b) False

Chapter 12 Review

Dorian encounters Basil on his way home from a party. Although he tries to ignore Basil on the street, the painter calls out and engages him in conversation. Basil says that he just left Dorian's home after waiting for hours, and he's relieved to have run into him on the street. He confides that he is leaving on a trip and wanted to speak with Dorian before his departure. Dorian invites him inside.

As the men converse. Basil admits that he is very concerned over the gossip he has been hearing about Dorian and pushes him to explain why so many of his friendships have ended in disaster. Dorian hedges, and Basil wonders aloud whether he knows his friend at all. He wishes that he could see Dorian's soul but notes, "only God can do that." Dorian reacts with a bitter laugh and offers to show Basil the diary of his soul. He grabs a lamp and leads his friend up the stairs to the schoolroom.

Discussion Topics:

1. Why does Basil visit Dorian?
2. What crimes does Basil accuse Dorian of committing?
3. Do you believe that Basil still cares about Dorian? Explain.

Chapter Quiz:

12.01: During the conversation between Dorian and Basil, the artist expressed concern about...
a) his own poor health
b) his worry that he might run low on money during his trip
c) whether Dorian would ever find happiness in marriage and produce an heir
d) Dorian's reputation

12.02: What views did Basil reveal in this chapter about position and wealth?
a) Position and wealth are not everything in life; reputation matters.
b) The richer and more prominent you are, the more pleasure you can pack into your life.
c) To an artist, nothing in life matters except creating art.
d) Power and wealth corrupt, so he shunned both during his life.

12.03: When Basil informed Dorian that he would be taking a trip for six months, where did he say he was going?
a) Munich
b) Dublin
c) Paris
d) America

12.04: Dorian tells Basil that he keeps a daily diary of his life? What form does it take?
a) the portrait Basil painted of him
b) a leather-bound journal
c) writing down day-to-day events on scraps of paper
d) notes dictated at the end of each day to his personal servant, Victor

12.05: In Chapter 12, where does Dorian lead Basil?
a) a tavern where they have a drink to celebrate Basil's upcoming trip
b) upstairs to the attic to show him the portrait
c) the theater where Sibyl had performed before she took her life
d) to Lord Henry's carriage

12.06: What did Basil say he planned to do during the six months he would be away?
a) drink, party, and go to brothels
b) shut himself up in a studio and start painting a new masterpiece
c) spend some time taking care of his aging parents
d) try to sell a dozen of his paintings to major museums to help fund his extravagant lifestyle

12.07: What is the date when Chapter 12 opens?
a) November 9th, the eve of Dorian's birthday
b) Friday the 13th
c) Christmas Eve
d) New Year's Day

12.08: How old is Dorian in Chapter 12?
a) 29
b) 33
c) 37
d) 39

12.09: What did Basil believe about the aesthetic of sin?
a) Some people can sin without consequence, while others suffer great punishments for small transgressions.
b) Sin is a moral judgment that varies from one society to another.
c) A man's actions are sinful only if they are done with evil intent.
d) Sin will show on a man's face. It cannot be concealed.

Chapter 13 Review

Dorian brings Basil inside the schoolroom and whispers for him to close the door. He tells Basil to pull the cover off the painting, but the painter thinks he is mad, so Dorian rips it off himself. Basil cannot believe what he sees. He recognizes his brushstrokes and colors in his painting, but the portrait has been horribly altered as if it were some foul parody. As Basil stares at the hideous sight, Dorian confides that his wish to remain young and beautiful while the painting ages had been granted. Shocked, Basil cannot believe that he painted such a monstrous thing. Dorian says it is the face of his soul and laments it is too late when Basil insists that they pray together. As rage grows within him, Dorian picks up a knife and stabs Basil repeatedly. He feels no emotion afterwards and calmly covers up the scene. He creates an alibi for himself and when he returns home, he looks up the address of a former friend named Alan Campbell.

Discussion Topics:

1. Describe what Basil sees when he looks at Dorian's portrait.

2. How does Basil react to the drastic changes in his painting?

3. Do you believe that Dorian is doomed at this point in the story, or can he redeem himself? Explain your reasoning.

4. Why does Dorian murder Basil?

Chapter Quiz:

13.01: In the old schoolroom where Dorian led Basil, the only furnishings in the room were: one chair, a table, a bookcase filled with books, two tapestries, an old piano, and a picture with a rug draped over it.

a) True
b) False

13.02: What did Basil see in the corner of the grotesque painting that Dorian showed him?

a) an occult symbol representative of the Devil
b) the date that he had completed the painting
c) a small section of the canvas with his signature cut out
d) his signature, traced in long letters of bright vermilion

13.03: What did Basil say when he saw the hideous portrait?
a) "What did you do to my painting?"
b) "Why did you keep sinning? Why did you not stop?"
c) "What does it mean?"
d) "Oh my God! We must burn the painting at once!"

13.04: How did Dorian explain the painting's terrible transformation?
a) He blamed Basil for casting an evil spell on the painting.
b) He blamed Lord Henry for casting an evil spell on the painting.
c) He confessed that he had wished long ago that he could retain his youth, while the painting aged; inexplicably, his wish came to pass.
d) Sibyl's spirit was causing the painting, to reflect his every sin.

13.05: What was Basil's observation when he pondered whether the painting was a true reflection of Dorian's life?
a) Dorian must repent and lead a solitary life in a Catholic monastery
b) Dorian should begin immediately doing good deeds to reverse the terrible painting, even if it meant that he himself would age.
c) If the painting was a reflection of what Dorian had done with his life, his character was even worse than the vile gossip about him.
d) None of these answers are correct.

13.06: What did Basil propose they should do to make things better?
a) Burn the painting.
b) Dorian should sit for another portrait to replace the first one.
c) They should never speak again, because Dorian was cursed.
d) They should pray together.

13.07: How did Dorian feel after he murdered Basil?
a) strangely calm
b) excited
c) sick to his stomach
d) furious, because he was still stuck with the dreadful painting

13.08: What was the name of Dorian's servant in this chapter?
a) Frederick
b) Francis
c) Francois
d) Franco

13.09: After Basil's murder, Dorian paced in his library and then looked up an address for...
a) the residence in Paris where Sibyl's mother was staying
b) a lawyer who had bailed Dorian out of trouble in the past
c) a young actress whom he had dated for several months
d) a man named Alan Campbell

Chapter 14 Review

The next day, Dorian awakens and remembers the terrible events of the night before. He gives a letter to his valet to deliver to Alan Campbell, summoning the man to his home. He picks up a book of poems to read as he reflects on his past relationship with Campbell. When the man arrives, Dorian confesses that there is a dead man upstairs, and he needs Campbell's help and knowledge of chemistry to dispose of the body. Campbell refuses. Dorian admits that he murdered Basil and must have help disposing of the evidence. He begs Campbell, who refuses to help.

Dorian picks up a piece of paper, writes something on it, and hands it to Campbell, who looks horrified as he reads it. He then pulls a letter from his pocket, shows the address to Campbell, and threatens to send it if the man does not help him. Campbell agrees, saying that he will need a few items from his home to dispose of the body. Dorian dispatches his servant to fetch the items. He then leads Campbell to the attic, where he sees that his portrait has become even more malevolent. He covers it quickly and Campbell asks him to leave the room. Locking the door, he goes to work. He emerges after several hours, insisting that he and Dorian must never meet again. When Dorian enters the schoolroom, Basil's body is gone and only the pungent odor of nitric acid remains.

Discussion Topics:

1. Who is Alan Campbell, and why does Dorian ask to meet with him?

2. After Dorian kills Basil, what changes appear in the portrait?

3. Why does Alan Campbell acquiesce to Dorian's vile demand?

4. The author never reveals what Dorian wrote on the piece of paper that he gave to Campbell, which convinced the man to help dispose of Basil's body. Imagine that you were able to look over Dorian's shoulder as he wrote the note—what did it say?

Chapter Quiz:

14.01: How many letters does Dorian sit down to write in Chapter 14?
a) One
b) Two
c) Three
d) Five

14.02: What does Dorian do with the letters that he wrote after he murdered Basil?

a) He put them in his mailbox.
b) He placed them on his desk in plain sight so they'll be found.
c) He gave one to his valet to deliver and put the others in his pocket.
d) He decided against sending the letters and tore them up.

14.03: What book caught Dorian's attention as he tried to get Basil's murder out of his mind?

a) Shakespeare's *Othello*
b) Gautier's *Emaux et Camees*
c) Poe's *The Pit and the Pendulum*
d) Poe's *The Raven*

14.04: How long had Dorian known Alan Campbell at this point in the story?

a) six months
b) two years
c) five years
d) many years, since childhood

14.05: Who does Dorian ask for help with disposing of Basil's corpse?

a) his servant, Francis
b) Lord Henry
c) his servant, Victor
d) Alan Campbell

14.06: After Dorian confesses to Basil's murder to Alan Campbell, the man feels sorry for him and agrees to help dispose of the body.

a) True
b) False

14.07: What common interest did Dorian share with Alan Campbell that led to their friendship?

a) drawing
b) music
c) theater
d) travel
e) coin collecting

14.08: What caused Dorian's friendship with Alan Campbell to sour?
a) The reason is not revealed in the story.
b) Campbell chastised Dorian after Sibyl killed herself.
c) They had a drunken argument one night at a local tavern.
d) Dorian felt that Campbell was too "common" to associate with.

14.09: How did Campbell respond to Dorian's plea for help disposing of Basil's body?
a) He agreed but to help, but he demanded that Dorian pay a large sum of money for his assistance.
b) He offered to help but said Dorian would owe him a huge favor that he would collect one day.
c) He agreed to help but only after Dorian threatened to kill him.
d) Campbell refused.

14.10: How did Dorian explain Basil's death to Alan Campbell?
a) He and Basil had argued; Basil had attacked him with a knife, and he defended himself.
b) A robber broke into Dorian's late at night and killed Basil.
c) Basil committed suicide because he was despondent over money and lack of artistic motivation.
d) The two men had spent the night with a prostitute, who stabbed Basil because he would not pay her.

14.11: Dorian passed a note that he had written to Alan Campbell—what did the note say?
a) It was Dorian's confession to Basil's murder.
b) It broadly confessed to all of the sins and misdeeds that Dorian had committed over the years.
c) The story does not reveal what the note says.
d) It explained that Basil's painting had cursed his life and caused him to sink into a morass of evil.

14.12: After Alan Campbell refused to help, Dorian told the man that he had a letter in his pocket he wrote that morning with incriminating information about Campbell, and he threatens to mail it if the man does not help him dispose of Basil's body.
a) True
b) False

14.13: What strange feature suddenly appears in the painting when Dorian looks at it as he is talking to Alan Campbell?

a) Dorian's eyes in the portrait are closed, and he appears to be dead.

b) Dorian's hand in the painting is covered in blood.

c) Dorian's mouth is twisted into a demonic smile, his eyes are glowing blood red.

d) Dorian's image has completely vanished from the painting, leaving a blank canvas.

14.14: What finally happens to Basil's corpse?

a) It is locked in a closet in the old schoolroom.

b) It is buried in the garden behind Dorian's house.

c) It is dissolved in acid.

d) It is thrown into a canal with a rock tied to Basil's ankle to make sure the body sinks to the bottom.

14.15: What did Campbell say to Dorian as he left?

a) He threatened to go to the police with Dorian's confession that he had murdered Basil.

b) He shouted at Dorian: "You are evil, and your soul will burn in hell."

c) He said, "I will pray for you."

d) He insisted that he and Dorian must never meet or talk again.

14.16: When Dorian returns to the schoolroom after biding Campbell farewell, what smell was in the air?

a) burnt flesh

b) nitric acid

c) vomit

d) burnt wood

Chapter 15 Review

That evening, Dorian attends a dinner party, which he views as more of a chore than an enjoyable event. Yet, he also delights in the morbid pleasure of his double life. Lord Henry arrives, and the guests gossip at length, discussing philosophies on women and relationships. Dorian leaves the party early. When he arrives home, he pulls Basil's personal effects from their hiding place and burns them. Then, he opens an ornate cabinet, brings out a canister of a pungent green, waxy substance, and smiles. He dresses and quietly leaves the house. Flagging a driver with a good horse, he asks to be taken to a remote location by the river.

Discussion Topics:

1. Lady Narborough confides that she is happy she did not meet Dorian Gray when she was younger. Why do you think she said this?

2. Explain how dramatic irony works in the scene of Lord Henry and Dorian dining at Lady Narborough's home.

3. Identify the speaker and explain the passage: "Nowadays all the married men live like bachelors, and all bachelors like married men."

4. What question was Dorian asked in this chapter that made him uncomfortable?

5. What does this phrase mean: "throw one's bonnet over the windmill"?

Chapter Quiz:

15.01: What word did both Lady Narborough and Dorian use to describe the dinner party?

a) treacherous

b) trite

c) tedious

d) terrible

15.02: What was Lady Narborough's reason for being glad that she had not met Dorian when she was younger?

a) She would have been crazy and fallen in love with him.

b) She would have hated his guts.

c) She would have felt threatened by his position and wealth.

d) She did not give a reason in the story.

15.03: Who arrived late to Lady Narborough's party?
a) Dorian
b) Lord Henry
c) Lady Henry
d) Lord Narborough

15.04: Who left Lady Narborough's party early?
a) Lord Henry
b) Lady Narborough herself
c) Dorian
d) No one left the party early.

15.05: What did Dorian do when he returned home after Lady Narborough's party?
a) He wrote a letter confessing to Basil's murder.
b) He wrote a love letter to Lady Narborough.
c) He burned Basil's bag and coat in the fireplace.
d) He ate dinner and drank himself to sleep.

15.06: What was inside the ornate canister described in Chapter 15?
a) a strong-smelling, green, pasty wax substance
b) a foul-smelling, red fluid resembling blood
c) a vial of holy water and a second vial of salt
d) a silver ring adorned with an occult symbol

15.07: After returning from Lady Narborough's party, what time did Dorian leave home to go back out that night?
a) midnight
b) 10 p.m.
c) 2 in the morning
d) around noon

Chapter 16 Review

As Dorian travels to a seedy opium den on the outskirts of town, he repeats over and over in his head what Lord Henry had told him on the day they met—about curing the soul by means of the senses, and curing the senses by means of the soul. He arrives at his destination, a filthy club packed with desperate people. He recognizes a man named Adrian and invites him to the bar for a drink. Although he had paid the women at the club not to speak to him, as he leaves the bar, a loud woman insults him and calls him Prince Charming, the pet name his female lovers use.

Outside, Dorian encounters James Vane in a dark alley. Vane holds a gun to Dorian's head, identifies himself as Sibyl's brother, and says he is going to kill him. Dorian slyly asks the man when his sister died, and when Vane replied eighteen years ago, Dorian told him to take him into the light and look at his face, which would prove that he was too young to have been involved with Vane's sister. Horrified by his mistake, Vane releases Dorian and returns to the bar. The loud woman asked why James didn't kill Dorian and said he had ruined her life eighteen years ago. James ran back out to the street to kill Dorian, but he was gone.

Discussion Topics:

1. What does Dorian say he most needs to do?
2. Where does Dorian go to forget his troubles?
3. Describe how Dorian ruined James Vane's life.
4. How does Dorian manage to escape from James Vane?

Chapter Quiz:

16.01: When Dorian left his home after Lady Narborough's party, where was he going?
a) a local tavern
b) an opium den
c) a brothel
d) Lord Henry's estate

16.02: Dorian went to an opium bar hoping to drug himself in a stupor and possibly find someone to take Sibyl Vane's place in his lonely life.
a) True
b) False

16.03: What happened to Dorian after he left the opium den?
a) He ran into Sibyl Vane's brother.
b) He ran into Lady Henry.
c) He tripped and fell into a gutter.
d) He encountered a prostitute and paid her to come home with him for the night.

16.04: When James Vane confronts Dorian in an alley outside of the opium den, what did he say?
a) He accused Dorian of killing his sister, and he was scum of the earth.
b) He asked Dorian to explain what happened the night his sister died.
c) He had gone to the police to lodge murder charges, but they refused to prosecute.
d) He had been searching for Dorian for years, but only knew the pet name that his female lovers called him.

16.05: How did Dorian convince James Vane that he could not be the man who was involved with his sister?
a) He showed Vane his passport, proving that he was in America at the time Sibyl took her life.
b) He told James to look at his face—he was far too young to be the man that Vane was looking for.
c) He said that he had lived in Paris until two years ago, so he could not possibly have known Vane's sister.
d) None of these answers are correct.

16.06: What did James threaten to do to Dorian?
a) rip him apart limb by limb
b) beat him up and put him in the hospital
c) pray for him
d) report Dorian's crimes to the police
e) Write a tell-all book exposing Dorian as a sociopath.

16.07: When Dorian encounters James Vane in Chapter 16, how long had it been since Sibyl's death?
a) 10 years
b) 3 years
c) 15 years
d) 18 years

16.08: Did James Vane believe Dorian's excuse that he could not be the man who was involved with his sister?

a) Yes

b) No

16.09: What happened after James Vane let Dorian go that made him realize Dorian was indeed the man he was seeking?

a) A bartender told him that Dorian had lived in the town since birth.

b) He realized that the birthdate on Dorian's passport made him older than he looked and claimed to be.

c) A woman from the bar told James that eighteen years ago, Dorian had ruined her life.

d) A waitress told him that Dorian made a rude gesture as he walked away.

Chapter 17 Review

Dorian throws a gala party and enjoys a lively conversation with the duchess and Lord Henry. They opine on the value of beauty and love. The duchess says she must depart to dress for dinner, and Dorian offers to pick some orchids from the observatory. After he departs, Lord Henry chastises the duchess for her flirtations. Dorian is gone for quite a while, which causes them to worry, and they go look for him. When they find him, he is lying on the floor, having apparently fainted.

When Dorian comes to and manages to get to his feet, he assures them that he is fine, but he does not explain how he ended up on the floor. He insists on dressing and coming to dinner, despite Lord Henry's protest. As Dorian dresses for dinner, he remembers the face of James Vane glaring at him through a window in the observatory.

Discussion Topics:

1. According to Lord Henry, why are reputations important?

2. Why does Dorian go into hiding throughout this chapter?

3. Identify the speaker and explain the passage: "Courage has passed from men to women. It is a new experience for us."

4. Lord Henry said: "To define is to limit." What does he mean?

5. Dorian's nickname for Lord Henry is Prince Paradox. What does that nickname imply about Lord Henry's personality and/or lifestyle?

Chapter Quiz:

17.01: On the night of Dorian's gala party, how much time has passed since Dorian encountered James Vane outside an opium den?

a) two days

b) three weeks

c) two months

d) one week

17.02: How is Lord Henry related to the Duchess of Monmouth?

a) They are cousins.

b) They are brother and sister.

c) They are not related.

d) The Duchess is the adopted daughter of his wife's brother.

17.03: What was the first name of the Duchess of Monmouth?
a) Edith
b) Ethyl
c) Gladys
d) Gwendolyn

17.04: How many people were at Dorian's party in Chapter 17?
a) eight
b) twelve, and more were expected to arrive the next day
c) fifteen
d) more than twenty

17.05: According to Lord Henry, what made England what it is today?
a) tea, cricket, and the Queen
b) liquor, women, and history
c) beer, the Bible, and the seven deadly virtues
d) wine, women, and song

17.06: What kind of flower did Dorian go to pick for the Duchess of Monmouth?
a) roses
b) orchids
c) carnations
d) wildflowers

17.07: Why did Dorian faint in this chapter?
a) He saw James Vane's face glaring at him through the window.
b) He drank too much.
c) He lost consciousness because he had pneumonia.
d) He became light-headed after smoking opium in the garden.

Chapter 18 Review

Dorian spends the next day hiding inside the house, frightened because he had seen James Vane's face the night before. He is upset and in tears when Lord Henry visits him. He remains inside several more days before he convinces himself that his conscience had imagined Vane's face.

Finally, Dorian ventures outdoors and joins up with a group of guests who had gathered for a sport hunting event. As a man named Geoffrey raised his rifle to shoot at a rabbit. Dorian cried out for him not to shoot, but Geoffrey fired, hitting the hare, and shooting a man who had been hiding in the thicket. The man was quite dead from a gunshot wound to the chest.

Following the mishap, the shooting event was called off, and as Dorian accompanied Lord Henry back to the house, he lamented that the incident was a bad omen. Later, the gamekeeper came to inform Dorian that no one knew the dead man's identity, except that he was a sailor. Startled by this news, Dorian hurries out to view the bod and discovers that the dead man is James Vane.

Discussion Topics:

1. What happens during the sport hunting event Dorian attended?
2. Describe the hunters' reactions to a man being shot in the bushes.
3. How does Dorian feel about the death of James Vane?

Chapter Quiz:

18.01: How many days did Dorian stay inside his home after seeing the face of James Vane in the window?

a) one day
b) three days
c) a week
d) two weeks

18.02: When Dorian joined the party, what sport were the attendees engaging in?

a) horse racing
b) horseshoes
c) fencing
d) shooting

18.03: What happened when Geoffrey caught a hare in his sight and shot at it?

a) The gun misfired and exploded in his hands.
b) He killed the hare on the first shot.
c) He shot the hare as well as a man hiding in a nearby bush.
d) He fired, but nothing happened because his gun had no bullets.

18.04: When a man was killed during the sport hunting activity, what did Dorian think about the event?

a) It was a bad omen.
b) The injured man was a fool for hiding in the bushes.
c) He wondered what it would be like to shoot and kill a man.
d) He felt that the guests firing their rifles were buffoons and should have been more careful.

18.05: What fate befalls Sibyl Vane's brother, James?

a) He is killed by Dorian in a duel.
b) His ship is lost at sea in a violent storm.
c) He is accidentally shot by a hunter at Dorian's country estate.
d) He tries to shoot Dorian but fails, and he's sent to prison for attempted murder.

18.06: What did Lord Henry tell Dorian about the shooting accident to comfort him?

a) Accidents happen, it's no big deal.
b) It was the man's own fault for getting in front of the guns.
c) It was lucky that Dorian hadn't been the one who shot Geoffrey.
d) Geoffrey had bad karma and got shot because he deserved it.

18.07: After a man was accidentally killed at the party, the Duchess suggested the sport be halted for the rest of the day.

a) True
b) False

18.08: What did Dorian say he would do to be safe from James Vane?

a) pay someone to kill the man
b) find James Vane and make amends for his sins
c) travel to Paris and hide out in a monastery for a year
d) go away on a yacht

18.09: In Chapter 18, Dorian wrote a letter to Lord Henry. What did the letter say?

a) Dorian announced that he was going to the city to see his doctor and asked Lord Henry to entertain his guests while he was away.

b) Dorian confessed to the murder of Basil and said he was fleeing to another country to stay out of jail.

c) Dorian said that James Vane was stalking him and asked for his advice.

d) All of these answers are correct.

18.10: What did Dorian's head-keeper come to tell him about the man who had been shot by the sport hunters?

a) The man hiding in the bushes was stalking Duchess Gladys.

b) The man hiding in the bushes was lying in wait to kill Lord Henry.

c) No one at the party knew who the man was, but apparently, he was a sailor.

d) The man in the bushes had been hired by James Vane to kill Dorian.

18.11: Why was Dorian startled by the revelation that the man who was shot while hiding in the thicket might have been a sailor?

a) He was surprised anyone cared that a fool hiding in the bushes had been shot.

b) He thought it odd that a sailor had been invited to the party.

c) He feared that the stranger was a detective investigating Basil's sudden disappearance.

d) He wondered if the man could be James Vane.

18.12: Who was the stranger that Geoffrey shot in the bushes?

a) An assassin stalking the Duchess

b) A killer hired by James Vane

c) James Vane

d) The man's identity was not revealed in the story

Chapter 19 Review

Dorian vows to Lord Henry that he is going to change his life, and he already had done his first good deed by sparing the heart of a young girl who had fallen in love with him. Henry laughs at him, and Dorian changes the subject. He asks what is happening at the club lately, and Henry shares the latest gossip. The conversation turns to Basil's disappearance, and Dorian asks what would Henry think if he told him that he had murdered Basil. Henry said he would not believe it, as crimes of that nature are vulgar and far beneath Dorian. They talked at length about Basil, and Henry inquired about their relationship, observing that Basil had stopped being a good painter after he got involved with Dorian. He invites Dorian to join him at the club that evening to meet a young man who had requested an introduction. Dorian declines, but Lord Henry insists.

Discussion Topics:

1. After a lifetime of debauchery, Dorian decides to redeem himself and does right by a country girl he was seeing. Why does he want to change?

2. How serious is Dorian about redeeming himself? Explain.

3. Consider the saying: "What does it profit a man to gain the whole world and lose his soul?" How does this represent Lord Henry's final influence over Dorian?

4. Identify the speaker and explain the passage: "You are the type the age is searching for and what is afraid it has found."

Chapter Quiz:

19.01: Lord Henry says he does not believe Dorian could have killed Basil because the act of murder is too vulgar, and Dorian doesn't have it in him.
a) True
b) False

19.02: At this point in the story, how long has as Basil been missing?
a) ten days
b) six weeks
c) two months
d) six months

19.03: What news do we learn about Lord Henry's marriage?
a) His wife is dying and has one month to live.
b) Henry is dying and has one month to live.
c) He is getting divorced.
d) None of these answers are correct.

19.04: What does Lord Henry say about San Francisco?
a) It's a city that everyone falls in love with when they visit.
b) It's crime-infested, and the people living there are uncultured.
c) It's a very expensive city, and no one can afford to live there.
d) Everyone who disappears is reportedly seen in San Francisco; it's an odd thing.

19.05: Why does Lord Henry insist Dorian go to the club that night?
a) He wants to introduce someone to Dorian.
b) A birthday party is being held for Lord Henry.
c) He is having a birthday party for his wife.
d) He is celebrating his divorce and wants Dorian to join him.

19.06: What happens to Alan Campbell?
a) He committed suicide.
b) He disappears and is not mentioned again in the story.
c) He is killed by an assassin hired by Dorian.
d) He dies in a freak accident while horseback-riding in the woods.

19.07: What was the reason for Lord Henry getting divorced?
a) He was caught in bed with another woman.
b) His wife ran away with another man.
c) The reason for his divorce is not revealed in the story.

Chapter 20 Review

Dorian walks home, and as passersby whisper his name, he remembers the delight he used to feel in being recognized. But now, he wished that he was anonymous. He reflects on various memories and grows angry as he thinks back over his life. Upon returning home, Dorian heads upstairs. He grabs a mirror that Lord Henry had given him many years ago and breaks it. Moving towards the painting, he decides it is the last piece of evidence of his life, and it must be destroyed. He picks up the knife that he had used to kill Basil and thrusts it into the painting. A terrible crash brings the servants running, and when they enter the room, they find a hideously ugly old man with a knife in his heart, lying next to a portrait of a young, exquisitely handsome Dorian Gray

Discussion Topics:

1. What does Dorian do to his portrait, and what happens as a result?

2. Discuss the moral of this story in your own words?

3. Did Dorian have a chance for redemption at any point in this story, or was his fate sealed from the start? Explain your reasoning.

Chapter Quiz:

20.01: When Dorian checked the portrait to see if it had changed, what did he find?
a) The hideous face in the picture had softened, giving Dorian hope.
b) The portrait was unchanged.
c) The painting had disintegrated, freeing Dorian from its evil curse.
d) The painting was even more hideous, and the blood-red stain on the hand was even broader.

20.02: What did Dorian's servants find when they entered the old schoolroom?
a) Dorian was dead on the floor with a knife through his heart, and the painting was more grotesque than ever
b) Dorian was dead on the floor, still young looking, and the painting had disintegrated
c) A splendid portrait of Dorian, and a hideously ugly dead man on the floor with a knife in his heart
d) Both Dorian and the painting had vanished into thin air.

20.03: In the final chapter of the story, what does Dorian want most?
a) eternal youth
b) unlimited wealth
c) the freedom to pursue pleasure without consequence
d) a new life

20.04: When Dorian saw that the painting was even more deformed and grabbed the knife that he had used to murder Basil, what did he intend to do?
a) use the knife to kill himself
b) slash the terrible painting to shreds
c) use the knife that had killed the painter to kill the painter's work.
d) None of these answers are correct.

20.05: Who heard terrible screams coming from Dorian's house?
a) a next-door neighbor
b) two gentleman who happened to be walking by
c) a woman out for a stroll with her young child
d) Lord Henry, who was walking up the sidewalk to pay Dorian a visit

20.06: How did Dorian's servants enter the locked schoolroom?
a) They broke down the door.
b) They summoned the housekeeper who had a spare key to the room.
c) They had to go to the roof and drop down to the balcony.
d) A servant cut hole in the wall, allowing access to the room.

20.07: When Dorian went up to the schoolroom, he hoped to see that the portrait had changed to reflect his good deed and his resolve to change his ways.
a) True
b) False

20.08: How did the servants discern the identity of the dead man on the schoolroom floor?
a) Dorian had written a suicide note before stabbing himself in the heart
b) The corpse was wearing Dorian's rings.
c) When the local authorities arrived on scene, the body was identified as Dorian through fingerprints.
d) A blood sample drawn by the coroner matched Dorian's blood type.

20.09: As Dorian reflected on his past in the last chapter of the story, who or what are the two things he blamed for ruining his life?
a) his mother and father
b) Lord Henry and Basil
c) beauty and youth
d) ego and passion

Further Discussion/Essay Prompts

In addition to the suggested, chapter-based discussion/essay prompts given for each chapter in the preceding section, the following offer some further questions to consider with broader implications that pertain to the major developments in the story and its foundational premises and themes. Whether you are reading *The Picture of Dorian Gray* for enjoyment or you are a student reading the story for a course, think of these prompts as food for thought which may give you a deeper understanding and appreciation for the story.

1. What does the painting of Dorian Gray symbolize?

2. Is the book "moral," "immoral," or neither? Explain its ultimate message in your own words.

3. Lord Henry tells Dorian that beauty is a form of genius, yet he tells Basil genius lasts longer than beauty. Explain how both statements can be true and make sense, or why they are a hopeless contradiction.

4. Do you think Basil was right in not wanting Lord Henry to meet Dorian? Explain your reasoning.

5. While the story has Faustian overtones, Dorian Gray never signs a contract for his soul. He merely utters a wish: "If it were I who was to be always young and the picture that was to grow old! For that--for that--I would give everything! Yes, there is nothing in the whole world I would not give! I would give my soul for that!" Who granted Dorian's wish and thus represents the devil at this point in the story?

6. Lord Henry said: "Youth is the one thing worth having." Explain why you agree or disagree.

7. What happened to Dorian's parents?

8. Describe the relationship between Lord Henry and Dorian, and explain why Henry had such a profound effect on Dorian's life.

9. Describe Sibyl Vane and Dorian's impression of her.

10. Do you think Sibyl truly loved Dorian, or was she attracted to his wealth and position? Explain.

11. Was Wilde trying to influence readers' views through Henry's character? Have you changed any of your opinions on life since reading this story?

12. Lord Henry asks, "When is she Sibyl Vane?" and Dorian replies, "Never." Is Dorian in love with Sibyl or her acting? Explain.

13. What do you think Basil meant when he observed that the painting is the real Dorian Gray?

14. Is Wilde trying to portray Lord Henry in a positive or negative light? Explain.

15. Why do you think Dorian fell out of love with Sibyl when he attended a performance and saw her mediocre acting?

16. Do you believe Dorian was sincere in his letter to Sibyl or did he write what he thought she wanted to hear?

17. Why did Lord Henry became so deeply involved in Dorian's life?

18. What was the importance of Sibyl's character in this book?

19. Was Lord Henry a good friend to Dorian? Explain.

20. Why was Dorian afraid to show his painting to Basil?

21. Why do you think Dorian ignored the possibility of the portrait returning to normal if he became a better person?

22. What's the importance of the yellow book Lord Henry gave to Dorian?

23. Why did Dorian stow Basil's portrait in his attic?

24. Did Lord Henry and/or Basil have a significant role in what happened to Dorian? Explain.

25. What Dorian wrote in the letter to Alan Campbell is not divulged in the story. What do you think the letter might have said?

26. Why did the friendship between Dorian and Basil deteriorate as the story progressed?

27. Who do you believe is ultimately to blame for the corruption of Dorian's soul?

28. Why did Dorian finally decide to show Basil the horribly distorted painting?

29. After Basil saw the hideous portrait, why did Dorian react so violently after having dealt with the painting for so many years?

32. "People know the price of everything and the value of nothing." Do you believe this is true in today's world? Explain.

30. Basil once said to Dorian: "You have a wonderful influence. Let it be for good, not for evil." What do you think might have happened if Dorian had used his influence to help people instead of hurting people?

31. What did Basil mean when he said he "put too much of himself" into painting Dorian Gray's portrait?

33. Basil refers to Lord Henry is an extraordinary fellow who never does a wrong thing. Yet, he is deeply concerned about Henry influencing Dorian. Explain this apparent contradiction.

34. Lord Henry seems to believe that one must help himself before helping others. Explain why you agree or disagree with this philosophy?

35. Was Dorian evil? Explain your reasoning.

36. What if Basil had prevented Lord Henry from meeting Dorian? How do you think Dorian's life would have turned out?

37. As Dorian watched his portrait grow more and more grotesque, did he sometimes express pleasure at the terrifying transformation, and if so, why do you think he reacted that way?

38. Why do you think Basil asked Dorian for forgiveness after he saw his grotesque painting?

39. Why does Dorian explode in rage when Basil seeks forgiveness, and why does he have no remorse after murdering his long-time friend?

40. What does it say about Campbell's character that he submitted to Dorian's demand rather than being blackmailed?

41. Lady Narborough discusses how unfortunate her daughter's life is because she has seen no scandals. Do you think a scandal-free life is a good thing or bad? Explain.

42. Is Dorian responsible for the tragedies that befall the people around him? Is Lord Henry responsible for Dorian's ruined life? When is someone responsible for the actions of others around them?

43. Identify and discuss the symbols of innocence in the story.

44. Although the story is a dark tale of Dorian's sins and debauchery, did he ever have an opportunity for redemption? If so, what point in the story was his best opportunity?

45. If there had been one more scene in the book, and it recounted Lord Henry's next dinner party after Dorian's death, what pithy one-liner might he have said about the life and death of Dorian Gray?

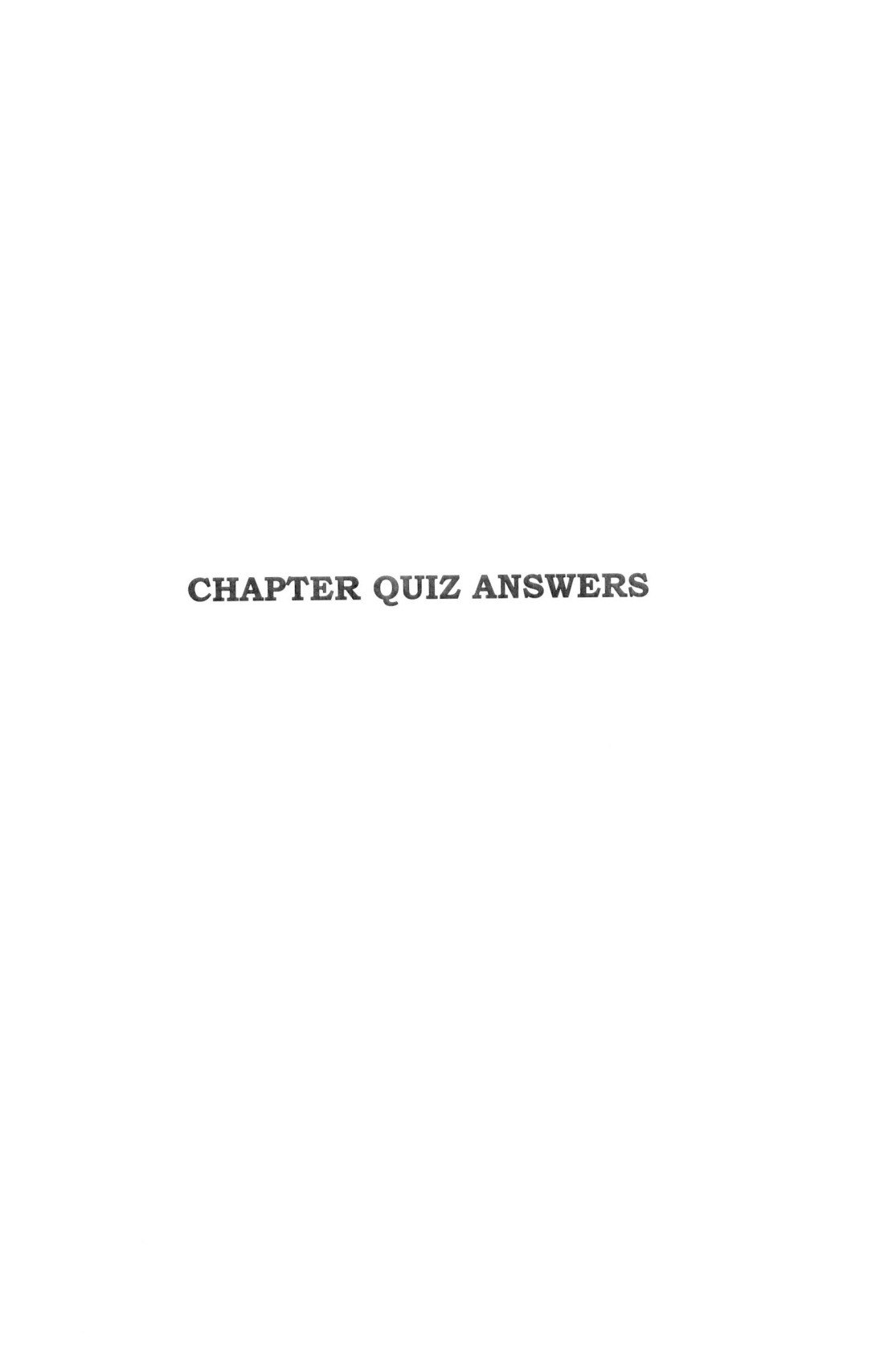

CHAPTER QUIZ ANSWERS

Chapter 1 Quiz: Answers

1.01: What does Basil request of Lord Henry when Dorian arrives at his studio?

b) He asks Lord Henry not to influence Dorian.

1.02: Who is Basil Hallward?

d) a well-known artist

1.03: What do Lord Basil and Lord Henry discuss in this chapter?

b) the subject of a beautiful painting created by Hallward

1.04: Why does Basil not want to exhibit his portrait of Dorian Gray?

a) Basil believes he has put too much of himself into the painting.

1.05: How does Basil initially meet Dorian?

d) at a party hosted by Lady Brandon

1.06: Dorian became an obsession for Basil, who declared that he was...

b) his sole inspiration

1.07: Basil sensed that despite his beauty, Dorian was on the verge of a terrible crisis.

a) True

1.08: In what location does the novel begin?

c) Basil Hallward's home

1.09: Dorian Gray's hair color is described as...

c) golden

Chapter 2 Quiz: Answers

2.01: Which one of the following statements is correct?
c) Basil warned Dorian that Lord Henry is a bad influence.

2.02: What is Lord Henry's personal philosophy?
b) The highest of all duties is the duty that one owes to one's self.

2.03: Lord Henry warned Dorian that...
a) Dorian's youth and beauty will quickly fade.

2.04: Basil urged Dorian to live life to its fullest and devote himself to seeking new sensations rather than pursuing common pastimes.
b) False

2.05: How did Lord Henry feel about Basil's finished portrait of Dorian?
d) He called it the finest thing of modern times.

2.06: Why was Dorian unhappy when he saw his finished portrait?
c) He lamented that the portrait would remain forever young, while he grows old.

2.07: What did Basil decide to do with the finished painting?
a) He gave it to Dorian Gray as a gift.

2.08: What stuns Dorian when he initially meets Lord Henry?
c) what Lord Henry says about youth

Chapter 3 Quiz: Answers

3.01: Who is Lord Henry's uncle?
b) Lord Fermor

3.02: What do Lord Henry and his uncle talk about in Chapter 3?
c) Dorian Gray's past

3.03: What happened to Dorian Gray's father?
d) He was killed just before Dorian was born.

3.04: What happened to Dorian Gray's mother?
a) She died soon after his birth.

3.05: Who raised Dorian Gray?
c) a loveless tyrant

3.06: How does Lord Henry react when he learns about Dorian's past?
a) He becomes increasingly fascinated with Dorian.

3.07: Who is Lord Henry's aunt?
b) Lady Agatha

3.08: What does Lord Henry speak about that shocks the group of socialites at lunch?
b) the virtues of hedonism and selfishness

3.09: Despite feeling appalled by Lord Henry, how do the socialite guests view him?
d) The guests feel he is clever, charming, and fascinating.

3.10: After the party, Dorian manages to spend more time with Lord Henry by inviting him to another party on the other side of town.
b) False

Chapter 4 Quiz: Answers

4.01: How many pictures did Lady Henry claim her husband had of Dorian?
b) 17, maybe 18

4.02: What was Lord Henry's belief about time?
a) Punctuality is the thief of time, and he is always late.

4.03: How did Dorian describe Lady Henry's dresses?
c) They looked as if they had been designed in a rage and put on in a tempest.

4.04: What did Lord Henry tell Dorian about marriage?
d) All of these answers are correct.

4.05: What news does Dorian share with Lord Henry in this chapter?
b) He tells him that he is in love.

4.06: Who is Dorian in love with?
a) Sibyl Vane

4.07: What is Lord Henry's response when Dorian claims Sibyl is a genius?
d) All of these answers are correct.

4.08: What is Sibyl Vane's occupation?
d) actress

4.09: How long has Dorian known Sibyl at this point in the story?
c) about three weeks

4.10: What play did Sibyl perform the night Dorian initially met her?
a) Romeo and Juliet

4.11: When did Dorian speak to Sibyl for the first time?
b) on the third night

4.12: How did Lord Henry describe Basil's personality?
a) Basil puts all that is charming about himself into his work, so he has nothing left for life but prejudices, principles, and common sense.

4.13: How often does Dorian go to watch Sibyl perform?
a) He goes every night.

4.14: When Lord Henry arrived home about half-past midnight, he saw a telegram lying on the hall table from Dorian. What did it say?
a) Dorian announced his engagement to marry Sibyl Vane.

Chapter 5 Quiz: Answers

5.01: What did Sibyl talk about on her walk with James?
a) She predicted that he would find great love and riches in Australia.

5.02: How much money did the Vane family owe to Mr. Isaacs?
a) 50 pounds

5.03: Who is James Vane to Sibyl?
b) her brother

5.04: What did Sibyl's mother say about happiness?
c) She was only happy when she saw her daughter act, and Sibyl should think of nothing other than acting.

5.05: Where is James Vane planning to travel?
c) Australia

5.06: Why was James leery about taking Sibyl to walk in the park?
a) He was too shabby; only swell people walk in the park.

5.07: Why is James worried about leaving for Australia?
b) He doesn't believe his mother will watch over Sibyl properly.

5.08: What does James question his mother about in this chapter?
d) rumors about a mysterious man who comes to watch his sister perform every night

5.09: How was the sight of James and Sibyl walking together described?
b) He was like a common gardener walking with a rose.

5.10: Which sibling is older: Sibyl or James?
a) James is younger than Sibyl.

5.11: How old is James in this chapter?
b) 16

5.12: What was James brooding about during his walk with Sibyl?
c) the mysterious suiter courting his sister and their mother's inability to protect her

5.13: After walking with Sibyl in the park, what question did James ask their mother over dinner?
b) Was his mother ever married to his father?

Chapter 6 Quiz: Answers

6.01: What news did Lord Henry share with Basil at dinner?
a) Dorian Gray was engaged to be married.

6.02: Why did Basil think that Dorian's engagement was absurd?
d) He believed Dorian should not marry someone so beneath him.

6.03: Why does Lord Henry say that being unselfish is a bad thing?
c) Unselfish people are boring and lack individuality.

6.04: What did Lord Henry expect would happen with Dorian and Sibyl?
a) Dorian would marry Sibyl for six months and become infatuated with someone else.

6.05: Basil appeals to Dorian because he represents all the sins that Dorian has never had the courage to commit.
b) False

Chapter 7 Quiz: Answers

7.01: What is the temperature in the theater on the night recounted in this chapter?
b) It was very hot.

7.02: What did Basil and Lord Henry think of Sibyl when they saw her perform?
c) She was quite beautiful, but she couldn't act.

7.03: After Sibyl's performance, Dorian said: "Last night she was a great artist. This evening, she is merely a commonplace mediocre actress."
a) True

7.04: What happened in this chapter after the second act of the play?
c) Lord Henry and Basil left early because they could not bear to watch Sibyl's mediocre performance any longer.

7.05: When Sibyl announced that her acting career was over, Dorian realized that he was in love with her talent and with the characters she played, not with Sibyl herself.
a) True

7.06: How did Dorian respond to Sibyl saying that her acting career was over?
c) He was embarrassed, disappointed, and upset: "You have killed my love," he declared.

7.07: How did Sibyl respond to Dorian's anger?
c) She cried and threw herself at his feet, begging Dorian not to leave her.

7.08: How did Dorian feel about Sibyl's tears?
c) Her tears annoyed him.

7.09: What was Sibyl's explanation for her bad acting?
d) Her characters and their emotions no longer interested her because she had fallen in love.

7.10: After Dorian expressed dismay over Sibyl's performance, what did he notice about the painting when he returned home that night?
b) The expression in the painting seemed different; there was a touch of cruelty to the mouth.

7.11: After reflecting on his harsh treatment of Sibyl, what did Dorian decide to do?

a) Stop listening to Lord Henry's poisonous theories and try to make amends to Sibyl

7.12: How did Lord Henry compare art to love?

d) Art and love are simply forms of imitation.

Chapter 8 Quiz: Answers

8.01: The day after Dorian's harsh reaction to Sibyl's performance, what time did he awaken?
b) well past noon

8.02: When Dorian awoke and examined the painting again, what did he notice?
b) His portrait had changed, and the expression seemed even more cruel than it was the night before.

8.03: After much reflection on the painting, to whom did Dorian write a letter?
c) Sibyl

8.04: Who knocked at the door as Dorian finished writing a letter?
a) Lord Henry

8.05: When Dorian told Lord Henry that he had caused a dreadful scene with Sibyl the night before, but he was determined to make amends and marry her, Henry laughed and said Dorian was too worried about things which would be of little consequence when he looks back over his life.
b) False

8.06: What did Dorian think of Lord Henry's advice on life, relationships, and his ill-fated romance with Sibyl after her death?
b) He felt relief and thanked Lord Henry for being his best friend.

8.07: After Sibyl's death, who convinces Dorian to avoid becoming involved in the investigation?
d) Lord Henry

8.08: Lord Henry was concerned about Sibyl's death because he feared that an inquest might be held, and it would be unwise for Basil and his painting to be mixed up in a scandal.
b) False

8.09: How did Sibyl die?
c) She was found dead on the floor of her dressing room at the theater after ingesting a poisonous substance.

8.10: Why did Lord Henry advise Dorian not to waste tears over Sibyl?
a) She was less real than the characters she played in her acting.

Chapter 9 Quiz: Answers

9.01: What did Dorian say about emotion?
b) He did not want to be at the mercy of emotions; he wanted to use, enjoy, and dominate them.

9.02: What upset Basil about Dorian's reaction to Sibyl's death was that Lord Henry had exerted such a strong influence over someone who used to be so simple, natural, and affectionate.
a) True

9.03: Did Dorian get caught up in the investigation of Sibyl's death?
b) No, Sibyl did not even know Dorian's real name.

9.04: Dorian asked Basil to paint a portrait of...
c) Sibyl

9.05: Basil declared that he would never paint another portrait of Dorian, even though Dorian was eager to sit for him again.
b) False

9.06: How did Dorian respond to Basil's request to sit for him again?
d) He refused, saying that he could never sit for Basil again.

9.07: When Dorian asked Basil why he had refused to exhibit his portrait, Basil answered:
b) "Dorian, if I told you, you might like me less than you do, and you would certainly laugh at me."

9.08: What secret did Basil reveal to Dorian in this chapter?
a) He confided that he previously had drawn Dorian in many settings and ultimately created the most beautiful portrait he had ever drawn. Because of his emotion and the realism of the method, he had put too much of himself into Dorian's painting.

Chapter 10 Quiz: Answers

10.01: What did Dorian ask the housekeeper, Mrs. Leaf, to fetch for him in this chapter?
a) the key to the old, attic schoolroom

10.02: What was name of the servant with whom Dorian conversed in the first paragraph of this chapter?
d) Victor

10.03: What task did Mr. Hubbard and his assistant help Dorian with?
b) They carried the painting upstairs into the attic schoolroom.

10.04: What did Dorian find with his tray of tea in the evening?
b) a yellow book, a newspaper, and a letter from Lord Henry

10.05: As Dorian looked over the newspaper in this chapter, what passage did he find circled in red ink?
d) an article about the inquest into Sibyl Vane's death

10.06: Why was Dorian late to meet Lord Henry?
c) He lost track of time after becoming absorbed in the yellow book.

10.07: Why did Dorian feel brief remorse that he had not confided to Basil the reason that he wanted to hide the portrait?
a) He knew Basil's love for him was noble and intellectual, and the artist would have helped him resist Lord Henry's influence and the more poisonous influences that came from his own temperament.

10.08: Which description fits Mr. Hubbard, the frame-maker of South Audley Street?
c) a florid, red-whiskered little man

10.09: When Dorian decides that no one other than himself will ever see his portrait again, what does he do with the painting?
a) He hides it in the old schoolroom in his house.

10.10: What gift from Lord Henry has a profound influence on Dorian?
c) a book

Chapter 11 Quiz: Answers

11.01: What did Dorian often do when he returned from his mysterious absences?
d) He went up to the schoolroom and stood with a mirror in front of his portrait.

11.02: What did Dorian do once or twice a month in the winter and on Wednesday's throughout the season?
a) He held dinner parties featuring celebrated musicians in his home.

11.03: What interests did Dorian pursue in the years after Sibyl's death?
a) Catholicism, Darwinism, perfumes, music, and building collections of items with historical significance.

11.04: Why did Dorian have so many collections of great treasures?
b) The beautiful items in his home afforded him an escape from the degradation of his life.

11.05: How did Dorian feel as he often sat in front of the portrait?
a) He felt loathing, but also pride in his individualism.

11.06: Dorian curtailed his travels because he was fearful that someone might discover Basil's painting while he was away from home.
a) True

11.07: What happened to Dorian's reputation because of his travels and disappearances?
c) He became the object of gossip and mistrust.

11.08: How did Dorian feel about the gossip swirling around him?
c) He was unphased and felt that while gossip hurt him in the eyes of some, it raised his status to others.

11.09: The yellow book that Dorian received from Lord Henry made him view evil simply as a mode through which he could realize his conception of the beautiful.
a) True

Chapter 12 Quiz: Answers

12.01: During the conversation between Dorian and Basil, the artist expressed concern about...
d) Dorian's reputation

12.02: What views did Basil reveal in this chapter about position and wealth?
a) Position and wealth are not everything in life; reputation matters.

12.03: When Basil informed Dorian that he would be taking a trip for six months, where did he say he was going?
c) Paris

12.04: Dorian tells Basil that he keeps a daily diary of his life? What form does it take?
a) the portrait Basil painted of him

12.05: In Chapter 12, where does Dorian lead Basil?
b) upstairs to the attic to show him the portrait

12.06: What did Basil say he planned to do during the six months he would be away?
b) shut himself up in a studio and start painting a new masterpiece

12.07: What is the date when Chapter 12 opens?
a) November 9th, the eve of Dorian's birthday

12.08: How old is Dorian in Chapter 12?
c) 37

12.09: What did Basil believe about the aesthetic of sin?
d) Sin will show on a man's face. It cannot be concealed.

Chapter 13 Quiz: Answers

13.01: In the old schoolroom where Dorian led Basil, the only furnishings in the room were: one chair, a table, a bookcase filled with books, two tapestries, an old piano, and a picture with a rug draped over it.
b) False

13.02: What did Basil see in the corner of the grotesque painting that Dorian showed him?
d) his signature, traced in long letters of bright vermilion

13.03: What did Basil say when he saw the hideous portrait?
c) "What does it mean?"

13.04: How did Dorian explain the terrible transformation of the painting to Basil?
c) He confessed that he had wished long ago that he could retain his youth, while the painting aged; inexplicably, his wish came to pass.

13.05: What was Basil's observation when he pondered whether the painting was a true reflection of Dorian's life?
c) If the painting was a reflection of what Dorian had done with his life, his character was even worse than the vile gossip about him.

13.06: What did Basil propose that they should do to make things better?
d) They should pray together.

13.07: How did Dorian feel after he murdered Basil?
a) strangely calm

13.08: What was the name of Dorian's servant in this chapter?
b) Francis

13.09: After Basil's murder, Dorian paced in his library and then looked up an address for...
d) a man named Alan Campbell

Chapter 14 Quiz: Answers

14.01: How many letters does Dorian sit down to write in Chapter 14?
b) Two

14.02: What does Dorian do with the letters he writes after murdering Basil?
c) He gave one to his valet to deliver and put the others in his pocket.

14.03: What book caught Dorian's attention as he tried to get Basil's murder out of his mind?
b) Gautier's *Emaux et Camees*

14.04: How long had Dorian known Alan Campbell at this point in the story?
c) five years

14.05: Who does Dorian ask for help with disposing of Basil's corpse?
d) Alan Campbell

14.06: After Dorian confesses to Basil's murder, Campbell feels sorry for him and agrees to help dispose of the body.
b) False

14.07: What common interest did Dorian share with Alan Campbell that led to their friendship?
b) music

14.08: What caused Dorian's friendship with Alan Campbell to sour?
a) The reason is not revealed in the story.

14.09: How did Campbell respond to Dorian's plea for help disposing of Basil's body?
d) Campbell refused.

14.10: How did Dorian explain Basil's death to Alan Campbell?
c) Basil committed suicide because he was despondent over money.

14.11: Dorian passed a note to Alan Campbell—what did the note say?
c) The story does not reveal what the note says.

14.12: After Alan Campbell refuses to help, Dorian tells the man that he has a letter in his pocket he wrote that morning with information about Campbell, and he threatens to mail it if the man does not help him dispose of Basil's body.

a) True

14.13: What strange feature suddenly appears in the painting when Dorian looks at it as he is talking to Alan Campbell?

b) Dorian's hand in the painting is covered in blood.

14.14: What finally happens to Basil's corpse?

c) It is dissolved in acid.

14.15: What did Campbell say to Dorian as he left?

d) He insisted that he and Dorian must never meet or talk again.

14.16: When Dorian returns to the schoolroom after biding Campbell farewell, what smell was in the air?

b) nitric acid

Chapter 15 Quiz: Answers

15.01: What word did both Lady Narborough and Dorian use to describe the dinner party?
c) tedious

15.02: What was Lady Narborough's reason for being glad that she had not met Dorian when she was younger?
a) She would have been crazy and fallen in love with him.

15.03: Who arrived late to Lady Narborough's party?
b) Lord Henry

15.04: Who left Lady Narborough's party early?
c) Dorian

15.05: What did Dorian do when he returned home after Lady Narborough's party?
c) He burned Basil's bag and coat in the fireplace.

15.06: What was inside the ornate canister described in Chapter 15?
a) a strong-smelling, green, pasty wax substance

15.07: After returning from Lady Narborough's party, what time did Dorian leave home to go back out that night?
a) midnight

Chapter 16 Quiz: Answers

16.01: When Dorian left his home after Lady Narborough's party, where was he going?
b) an opium den

16.02: Dorian went to an opium bar hoping to drown himself in a stupor and possibly find someone to take Sibyl Vane's place in his lonely life.
b) False

16.03: What happened to Dorian after he left the opium den?
a) He ran into Sibyl Vane's brother.

16.04: When Dorian is confronted by Sibyl Vane's brother, what did the man say?
d) He had been searching for Dorian for years, but only knew the pet name that his female lovers called him.

16.05: How did Dorian convince James Vane that he could not be the man who was involved with his sister?
b) He told James to look at his face--he was far too young to be the man he was looking for.

16.06: What did James threaten to do to Dorian?
b) kill him

16.07: When Dorian encounters James Vane in Chapter 16, how long had it been since Sibyl's death?
d) 18 years

16.08: Did James Vane believe Dorian's excuse that he could not be the man who was involved with his sister?
a) Yes

16.09: What happened after James Vane let Dorian go that made him realize Dorian was indeed the man he was seeking?
c) A woman from the bar told James that eighteen years ago, Dorian had ruined her life.

Chapter 17 Quiz: Answers

17.01: On the night of Dorian's gala party, how much time has passed since Dorian encountered James Vane outside an opium den?
d) one week

17.02: How is Lord Henry related to the Duchess of Monmouth?
a) They are cousins.

17.03: What was the first name of the Duchess of Monmouth?
c) Gladys

17.04: How many people were at Dorian's party in Chapter 17?
b) twelve, and more were expected to arrive the next day

17.05: According to Lord Henry, what made England what it is today?
c) beer, the Bible, and the seven deadly virtues

17.06: What kind of flower did Dorian go to pick for the Duchess of Monmouth?
b) orchids

17.07: Why did Dorian faint in this chapter?
a) He saw James Vane's face glaring at him through the window.

Chapter 18 Quiz: Answers

18.01: How many days did Dorian stay inside his home after seeing the face of James Vane in the window?
b) three days

18.02: When Dorian joined the party, what sport were the attendees engaging in?
d) shooting

18.03: What happened when Geoffrey caught a hare in his sight and shot at it?
c) He shot the hare as well as a man hiding in a nearby bush.

18.04: When a man was killed during the sport hunting activity, what did Dorian think about the event?
a) It was a bad omen.

18.05: What fate befalls Sibyl Vane's brother, James?
c) He is accidentally shot by a hunter at Dorian's country estate.

18.06: What did Lord Henry tell Dorian about the shooting accident to comfort him?
b) It was the man's own fault for getting in front of the guns.

18.07: After a man was accidentally killed at the party, the Duchess suggested the sport be halted for the rest of the day.
b) False

18.08: What did Dorian say he would do to be safe from James Vane?
d) go away on a yacht

18.09: In Chapter 18, Dorian wrote a letter to Lord Henry. What did the letter say?
a) Dorian announced that he was going to the city to see his doctor and asked Lord Henry to entertain his guests while he was away.

18.10: What did Dorian's head-keeper come to tell him about the man who had been shot by the sport hunters?
c) No one at the party knew who the man was, but apparently, he was a sailor.

18.11: Why was Dorian startled by the revelation that the man who was shot while hiding in the thicket might have been a sailor?
d) He wondered if the man could be James Vane.

18.12: Who was the stranger that Geoffrey shot in the bushes?
c) James Vane

Chapter 19 Quiz: Answers

19.01: Lord Henry says he does not believe Dorian could have killed Basil because the act of murder is too vulgar, and he does not believe Dorian has that in him.
a) True

19.02: At this point in the story, how long has as Basil been missing?
b) six weeks

19.03: What news do we learn about Lord Henry's marriage?
c) He is getting divorced.

19.04: What does Lord Henry say about San Francisco?
d) Everyone who disappears is reportedly seen in San Francisco; it's an odd thing.

19.05: Why does Lord Henry insist Dorian go to the club that night?
a) He wants to introduce someone to Dorian.

19.06: What happens to Alan Campbell?
a) He committed suicide.

19.07: What was the reason for Lord Henry getting divorced?
b) His wife ran away with another man.

Chapter 20 Quiz: Answers

20.01: When Dorian checked the portrait to see if it had changed, what did he find?
d) The painting was even more hideous, and the blood-red stain on the hand was even broader.

20.02: What did Dorian's servants find when they entered the old schoolroom?
c) A splendid portrait of Dorian, and a hideously ugly dead man on the floor with a knife in his heart

20.03: In the final chapter of the story, what does Dorian want most?
d) a new life

20.04: When Dorian saw that the painting was even more deformed and grabbed the knife that he had used to murder Basil, what did he intend to do?
c) use the knife that had killed the painter to kill the painter's work.

20.05: Who heard terrible screams coming from Dorian's house in this chapter?
b) two gentleman who happened to be walking by

20.06: How did Dorian's servants enter the locked schoolroom?
c) They had to go to the roof and drop down to the balcony.

20.07: When Dorian went up to the schoolroom, he hoped to see that the portrait had changed to reflect his good deed and his resolve to change his ways.
a) True

20.08: How did the servants discern the identity of the dead man on the schoolroom floor?
b) The corpse was wearing Dorian's rings.

20.09: As Dorian reflected on his past in the last chapter of the story, who or what are the two things he blamed for ruining his life?
c) beauty and youth

-end-

Notes

Notes

Notes

Notes

Notes